Kafka's Son

THE HUNGARIAN LIST

SZILÁRD BORBÉLY

Kafka's Son

TRANSLATED BY
OTTILIE MULZET

LONDON NEW YORK CALCUTTA

The translator would like to thank the Hungarian Translators'
House, where this translation was partially completed, as well
as for their kind support through their Home Office
programme in 2020.

Seagull Books, 2023

Originally published in Hungarian as *Kafka fia*
© Suhrkamp Verlag Berlin, 2017
All rights reserved by and controlled through Suhrkamp Verlag Berlin

First published in English by Seagull Books, 2023
English translation © Ottilie Mulzet, 2023

ISBN   978 1 80309 268 3

British Library Cataloguing-in-Publication Data
A catalogue record for this book is available from the British Library

Typeset and designed by Seagull Books, Calcutta, India
Printed and bound by Hyam Enterprises, Calcutta, India

CONTENTS

A NOTE ON THE TEXT

The manuscript of *Kafka's Son*, as left by the author at the time of his death in 2014, had a title page but was clearly 'unfinished' in the sense of its partially fragmentary nature, including occasional incomplete or unfinished sentences, notes interpolated into the text, and so on. An endnote has been appended where sentences trail off, repeat or display inconsistencies.

Map of Prague, *c.* 1914, showing locations in the book

Belvedere Park

Čech Bridge

Zlatá ulička

Apartment 'Zum Schiff'

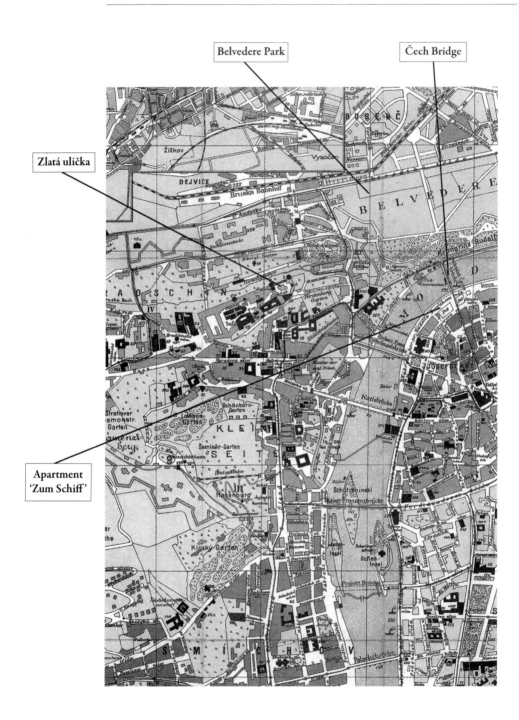

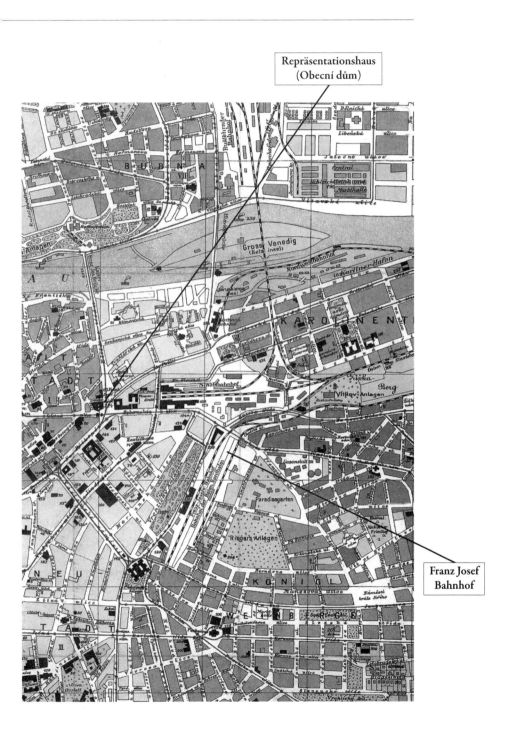

Repräsentationshaus
(Obecní dům)

Franz Josef
Bahnhof

To the Reader

This novel takes place in Eastern Europe. It is about journeys and those who journey. It is about the journeys of Franz Kafka, who is not identical with Franz Kafka. About staying in one place, without which travel would lose its meaning. And strolling, a trajectory that always doubles back upon itself; and the places that observe all of this, puzzled. They follow and accompany the one who strolls. The person who strolls along, never getting anywhere. He only gives structure to the places through his movement; he connects the places together. The spaces, which in Eastern Europe, no matter how crowded, are just as solitary as the person who intersects them with his strolling.

This book speaks of childhood, and therefore it is about those things which cast doubt upon space, that is to say, it speaks of a twin, which is the same thing. It speaks of how everyone has a twin, a twin born with him into the world. Everyone spends his most important years together with this likeness. Every game is played together. Then their paths diverge. For everyone ends up losing his twin, the reminder of whom henceforth becomes the mother. Of this, fathers know nothing. At such times, fathers are distant, retching from their hangovers in workplaces with crumbling walls, ears ringing, heads dizzy; they stare at the cigarette smoke of the taverns with expressionless faces, they march amid the changing terrain of Eastern Europe's battlefields, and they die quickly, divested of their illusions; or despairing, they remain alive, but knowing nothing at all of what this novel shall speak.

For this book speaks of that unbroken procession as sons become fathers in Eastern Europe and forget the reproaches against the world of their fathers that they themselves pronounced as children, as adolescents. They forget the clenched fist of their younger years, raised against the world of the fathers, shaken amid curses. Soon afterward, they used those same fists to beat those who shook their fists at them, beating them down into shreds of bloody flesh; their own fists now smooth, slavishly accepting the bribes tossed to them by their present masters. This book, therefore, speaks of words, words the fathers and sons exchanged with each other like battered farthings. It speaks of forgetting. That is to say, it speaks of me, the author of this book, who is not identical with myself, namely, it speaks of my twin. It speaks of how he set off one day upon the wings of words, although there was nothing urging him to do so. Rather, it was the opposite: the mute loss of his home in a country where he belonged nowhere. This occurred unconsciously before he would have known who he was, what writing was, or the people of writing. After his homelessness had become definitive, in the wake of an unexpected, yet even more inevitable tragedy, he set off in order to understand those with whom he had as little in common as with his own future. And so, to withstand his soul's pain, he escaped into imagination, to rewrite that past which had never been his home, just as it had never been his parents', whom he had lost. For whom he felt, evermore strongly over time, that he must tell this story. For his mother and his father. For his mother and his father: for Julia and Hermann, for whom there was only their past, and who now live eternally in the future. Amen.

* * *

When this book began, I still didn't know that my life would be a series of phases, ill-matched to each other. I watched the water as it flowed in the ditches. I watched the courtyard as it rose every spring, like dough from yeast, and the ground became filled with puddles. From that point on we crossed the courtyard only on planks. Then green moss appeared, as if a great piece of velvet had been laid down between the gate and the dung heap. It was a vivid green for a long time, nearly phosphorescent for a few days, then suddenly it disappeared. What remained became black, emitting a stench. The ground began to crack, plates of earth broken at the edges. We played with them, gathered them up. We are, therefore, somewhere in Eastern Europe, where on the swampy, impassable plains, slashed by water, the cackling from the necks of geese can be heard, the beating of their wings, as hissing, cackling, flapping, they raise great storms of dust, floundering, always frightened by something, falling from one panic into another, trampling each other down, they escape, these idiot beasts with their lovely heads.

Whenever I look at this picture my heart sinks. I know the fate of these geese growing fatter in the spring: hardly any of them will be alive by Christmas. According to tradition, St Martin's Day is the endpoint of their lives. After the happy days of spring, when they are pampered with nettles and hominy, after the rich pastures of early summer, the spring showers with their enormous bathing puddles, autumn arrives, when the geese, now grown big, are herded into a tiny hutch, although they can still squeeze their heads through the cracks between the wooden planks. Then autumn arrives, with its mud and frosts, the tumbleweed known as 'devil's wagon' and the gossamer of spider's webs, when even these proudly borne wings grow heavy; unlike domestic geese, they cannot fly.

These geese can only run or swim, but they no longer remember flight, and therefore when the time of the autumn rains comes to Eastern Europe, these birds, with their webbed feet, step easily across the muddy paths which draw all other creatures to themselves, making it impossible to ever escape from here.

The autumn brings their winter plumage to protect them from the night-time's wretched cold. But autumn also brings the hut, cobbled together from lathes and twigs, from dried sunflower stalks; the geese cannot waddle around inside, but they get used to it: they are fed with fresh cornmeal, pre-soaked to aid digestion and swollen, flavoured with small pieces of apple, and now they don't even want that, they can no longer move. They sit on the floor of the cage, once sprinkled with straw, now muddy and covered in goose shit. They stretch their heads out through the cracks: they don't need to stand to drink, the soaked cornmeal sits there in front of them. In their boredom, they just eat and eat. And when they don't have the strength to eat any more, or when they have had their fill, the time comes to stuff them. The women squeeze the geese between their legs, only the heads stretch upward to the height of the women's hands, so they can stuff them with the soaked cornmeal and apple mixture. The women's hands press the food down the geese's long necks down to the stomach. The geese will be even plumper, they make rattling sounds, they suffocate, the women are happy, because they know that the geese's livers will be even bigger and fatter. Then comes St Martin's Day, or for some of them Christmas, and they are slaughtered. Because this is the fate of geese in Eastern Europe. But not just that of geese, if I think about it.

From Hermann's Notes

The son is the absence of the father: everything suggested this ever since Franz had died. The first years were still easy, since like everyone who does battle with mourning, I lived out of spite. I didn't admit that God was right, God who took away my son, although I had been preparing for his death for a long time. Ever since that day, when, conquering his fears—perhaps because I'd been hounding him—he resolved to find a girl, and that strength in him, which until then had protected him from life, was annihilated. He would have said: that strength that protected him from me. And I would say: the strength that protected him from the Almighty, who created him to be so defenceless. Then, gathering all his strength, and conquering all his natural fears, in 1914 . . . he asked for Felice's hand,

The father is the grave of the son.
The son is life of the father. The father is the death of the son.

Kafka and the Streets

For a long time, the name of Kafka was just a merchant's name. Kafka was a merchant like so many others. At first, he was called Hermann. Then, during that time when he was well known for his city-centre shop, he changed it to Herrmann. In independent Czechoslovakia, after the war, he became Heřman to integrate better with his surroundings, evermore Czech and evermore nationally inclined. There was no problem with the name Kafka, as this was originally a Czech word meaning 'jackdaw'. Although, the *f* in the middle of the word looks like a mistake. It really should be a *v*. 'Kafka' sounds like the imitation of a voice, a kind of animal rattling in its throat, and only after that do the Czechs recognize the sounds, the human sounds. The original Czech word is *kavka* which means *csóka* in Hungarian and 'jackdaw' in English. As if wishing to recreate the jackdaw's voice, the hoarse throat-grinding and dull rasping sounds emitted by these clever birds. That is, according to the Czechs. Because the name of the same bird in Hungarian, *csóka*, lifts up that voice like a much more distant memory. This is made even more strange by the fact that this sound originates from a bird's throat, not a mammal's. Birds are much more distant from human beings. Their heads and their movements, no matter how daintily they cleave the air, remind one of reptiles and their ancestors, the dinosaurs. The expressionless eyes, their heads turning farcically round and the absence of a face give rise to fear in mammals. For us, birds seem to be fossilized, enchanted beings, petrified remnants of the ancient world. They may be flying fossils, but they are still fossils. This is also true of the jackdaw and the strange throat-rattle this black avian emits which people try to imitate: *kav-kav, kav-kav*. Kafka always thought of this gloomy sound when he evoked his father's name, with dread, within himself. The black jackdaw gambols across the ground all over Eastern Europe, hiding in bushes along the forest's edge, in the branches of tree-lined alleys separating the cultivated fields and the pastures. In Hungary, the jackdaw is the symbol of poverty. In the old days, people liked to catch them, and since they are clever birds, people would teach them some tricks. The Roma, who, as is well known, lived in Eastern Europe for long years like natural peoples, were close friends of the jackdaw. In the destitute winters, when the jackdaws could not find anything to eat, they learnt to recognize their mutual kinship. Neither the jackdaws nor the Roma ever wished to become merchants, unlike Herrmann Kafka. Because Herrmann Kafka always wanted to become a merchant.

In those days—at the end of the nineteenth century—to be a merchant, in economically deprived, poverty-ridden Eastern Europe, demanded, above all, an aptitude for austere, merciless thrift. Not frugality, but the ruthlessness of an exploitative miserliness. But it also meant silence and the knowledge of speech, as it had for millennia. Trade demands the clever knowledge of the use of words, not of enigmatic silence. It demands bargaining, which is perseverance itself. Bargaining is the forfeiture of language, the exchange of words. I give you a word, and you give me another in its place. I do not squander my words but preserve them. One had to be severe in economy to remain a merchant. Whoever could not obstinately persevere would not succeed. Hermann Kafka had a conspicuously tall physique. He was a resolute man of great strength. He had learnt to rely only upon his own strength. There are men who are made cold by solitude; later, they can never reveal their emotions. Someone who has lived through social exclusion will never dissolve into any kind of collective, even if accepted by it. Kafka came from the countryside to Prague, from the provinces to the city. He came from the south, going on foot, a journey where whatever he left behind, he destroyed. The bridges he crossed, the towns passing from hand to hand, the boarding houses where he stayed. And he built everything anew, by himself. He had to create everything anew. His shop, the goods within, his circle of acquaintances, the community of faith with the rabbi and the cantor, he created the street that he walked along every morning and after lunch. Kafka created Prague around himself. In the beginning he didn't know anything about Prague. He didn't even know the names, he didn't know what things were called. When he came to Prague for the first time, the city didn't even exist. Kafka said, let it exist. And behold. His son, Kafka, knew this very well. He knew that without his father Prague would never have existed, Hradschin would have never existed, Charles Bridge, the old city with its ghetto, its temples and towers. The figure of his tall and still-imposing father reminded Kafka, like an exclamation mark, of his own weakness. His large, cube-shaped head could be seen from far away as he walked to the shop. And his hair was trimmed short, delineating his skull with its cube-like shape even more clearly. Hermann was one of the building blocks of society, one of its trustworthy pillars. As opposed to Franz, who was more like the vault connecting the two pillars. This vault, however, was drawn only in imagination. And whoever traversed it was walking through nothing.

This novel takes place in Eastern Europe. In reality, it's not a novel and it doesn't take place anywhere. It doesn't relate events the way that novels usually do, it would only like to approximate that. In reality, it speaks of journeys. About the journeys of Kafka, who is not identical with Kafka. Namely, about staying in one place, without which travel would lose its meaning. In reality, of course, it's not even about Franz Kafka, the son, at all, it's much more about the father—about Kafka's father, the dreaded Hermann Kafka. Because sons usually understand the stories of their grandfathers. And conversely: in the stories of the grandsons, the grandfathers comprehend their own lives. Even more than that, it narrates a secret. It speaks of a rumour, a rumour about Kafka's son who perhaps never existed. It's a strange story, that much is sure. But as so often happens in novels, the author inevitably makes an appearance. So, in reality, it speaks of the author's childhood. About why he set off one day—to phrase it somewhat bombastically—upon the wings of words (if words have wings), although there was nothing prompting him to do so. Instead, the opposite: it was the mute loss of his home in a tiny village in Eastern Europe, where he had been cast by an accident of birth. In a country where, personally, he never belonged anywhere, and in which—due to circumstances beyond his control—he never would belong anywhere. He learnt this very quickly, somehow around the same time he learnt how to speak. That's why everything he read later on in Kafka's writings was so familiar to him. Then he also learnt that he could find a home in writing. Although this happened unconsciously, even before he could have known what writing was and who he was. Before he could have known anything about the people of the word. After his homelessness had become definitive—in the wake of an unexpected yet all-the-more inevitable tragedy—he set off on a journey through the pages of this novel to understand those with whom, just as with his own inescapable future, he had nothing in common. Perhaps he did so to endure his soul's pain. Because while he had learnt self-loathing, he nonetheless loved weighty words. He did not shield his readers from the pain of his protagonists which here, in Eastern Europe, is such a familiar experience. Just like that constant struggle with fate which turns heroes into tragic heroes against their will. That is why he too escaped into imagination, so that he could rewrite that past which was never his home, just as it had never been his parents' home, his parents who sunk without a trace in time. For the sake of whom he felt evermore strongly that this story must be told. For them. For himself. For Kafka's son: for the Father and the Son. Amen.

Kafka and My Twin

I must speak of my twin, who resembles me perfectly. He's almost a dead likeness for me. There's just one small difference between us: in my left eye, there's an irregular spot, like a tiny hole in the radial iris, whereas he has the same spot in his right eye. As if the eye had been pierced with a needle at one time. And the iris looks conspicuously like a target used by the archers of the steppes. They practice at twilight and their targets are grey. They glide along noiselessly on their short-legged horses, like falcons that hunt at night. Only the ones who close their eyes can hit the target as it merges into the first light of day. That's how it was with me and my twin. He had the very same spot in his right eye. We always knew exactly where the other was. The colour of our eyes was exactly the same. Both of us had grey eyes, like the lower part of a leaden spoon. We have such a spoon; we keep it in the flour tin. Our mother uses it to measure out the flour for making dough. When we were children, we liked to play with it. It was kept in the house in a windowless room that we called the larder, and in the larder there was a cupboard, and in the cupboard there was a tin box, and the tin box was where we stored the flour; it was a coloured tin box but with time the colours had worn off from the sides. You could still make out the name written on it years ago: Kafka. And if we looked closely, we could see another word: Bohemia. I had a particular liking for this word. Bohemia. It sounded like an excursion, or the name of a distant relative we'd known once. When our mother wasn't paying attention, we stole the spoon from the tin box. Sometimes we saw our own eyes in its grey-black depths. Once, my twin's eye somehow fell out and into the flour tin; it dropped down onto the leaden spoon. Just then our mother walked in. We were afraid of her, and so we quickly put the tin box back in its place. We pretended we were playing hide and seek. My twin hid beneath the chest of drawers, his face turned towards the ground. In this way, our mother didn't notice that his left eye had accidentally fallen into the flour tin, next to the leaden spoon. We couldn't think of anything else: I kept on counting, waiting for time to pass. We didn't dare tell our mother, who always got angry if one of us lost one of our body parts. Our mother was always terrified of this and fell into hysterics. Sometimes she even fainted. We didn't want her to get nervous for no good reason. She was looking for something in the wooden chest: it was taking a while. I kept on counting, I didn't know how long I would have to keep on counting. Suddenly, she found what she was looking for. Or at least I think so, because she picked something up and left the room. We quickly grabbed the flour tin, and blowing off the flour dust off the eyeball, I helped my twin slip it back into place. He kept his right eye closed so he wouldn't get scared.

I asked him if his eyeball had fallen out before.

It had. But, he begged me, don't tell our mother. He began to whimper like a dog when it suspects it will be punished. I saw that his trousers were moist in front, and on his left thigh a thin yellow vein ran down to his sandal. It was only then I took mercy on him, and I said: Of course, there's no way I would say anything, as long as you don't tell on me as well . . .

It only happened once, he said, I'd only turned over in bed. It was morning, I was looking out the window at the wrens on the trees. Maybe I strained my eyes too much. I don't know why it happened, my twin replied.

Never strain your eyes, and never try to remove it from its socket, I said to him, because then it will get loose and can fall out at any time. And never touch it with dirty hands, but surely you know this already.

It was just as you might have expected with a twin: whoever knows him thinks he is me. The two of us are present in every story. When my friends meet him on the street, they yell loudly. They greet him and speak to him as if continuing an interrupted conversation. My twin is prepared for this, and he doesn't want to let them down. So he pretends to be me.

This makes me uncertain, and sometimes I don't know if I am myself or my twin, because the same things that happen to him happen to me too, day after day. I myself don't know who those people are approaching me on the street: they begin explaining their troubled affairs, reminding me of my old, unfulfilled promises. I'm already used to this kind of pestering, yet still always surprised and fairly perplexed. Because the times when I was amused by playing a trick—pretending I understood everything—have long since passed. Now it just irritates me. And since at this point I only have very obscure memories of my twin—I was separated from him during a war in childhood, I don't remember why, maybe because the country's borders were redrawn, or there was some kind of internment—my memories seem evermore obscure. Sometimes, I'm not sure if my twin really existed, or if it was just a tale that people in my village somehow got me to believe.

Kafka in the Bathroom

This story begins in a bathroom. It's spring, or rather the end of spring. At such times, the earth gapes, its mouth opens wide. The entire earth is one big mouth: whether opened wide or completely closed is as yet undecided. Or it's not even a question of decision, but of point of view. In his childhood, the earth was still enchanted. It's Saturday: this will be significant later on in the story, when a certain book will turn up in the hands of the narrator. He selected it almost at random in the district library, where he always wanders in while waiting for the afternoon bus. He looks around and reads a bit. He knows how to hide amid the shelves and enjoy the silence. There's no silence anywhere else. The dictators of Eastern Europe always wanted to drive people insane and that is why silence was nationalized; silence, one of those vestiges of the ancient world. They took it out of circulation, just like the old money with the portraits of former dictators and their symbolic objects. They nationalized words as well, taking out the old words and putting new ones into circulation. The new words were much louder than the old words. The old words were forced back into the libraries, back in among the other old words, which either granted them a reprieve or simply failed to notice their presence.

He likes silence the best, but it is rare. Everywhere there is noise; machines and people alike are too loud. Where he lives, everyone is always yelling, always turning up the volume on the radio and listening to popular ballads. Many people sing along with the radio. They like televized entertainment, they laugh loudly and aggressively. They don't even pay attention, don't even want to understand the point of the joke. The mere appearance of a well-known comic is enough for them to start laughing with their entire body; it's more like guffawing, as bereft of spirit and meaning, they roar with laughter uncontrollably, sitting back in a lounge chair, sprawled on the bed. This guffawing is oppressive because the faces change, it's as if they aren't people any more. And he sees this sometimes outside too, on the long-distance buses that he uses to travel between his home, or rather his parents' home, and school. And in the classroom, he suffers from the same thing, he tries to avoid the conversations in the boys' bathroom and the hallways, the same jokes and ludicrous stories repeated ad nauseum. When school is over, he eats in the cafeteria. If he can, he arrives a little late, staying away from his classmates so he doesn't have to hear their conversations. He sits down as far away as he can from the others, at the end of the long table at the end of the lunchroom, swimming in grease. He doesn't cross the bleak concrete yard connecting the school and lunchroom, but circles the building, exits via the front entrance, then enters the dormitory yard from the street. There's more of a chance the others will have left the cafeteria already. He eats quickly and spar-ingly, trying to push aside the droplets of fat floating on the sur-face of the soup. The aluminium plate is battered and splotchy, with a cold film of opalescent grease. There are remnants of food spiced with paprika on the plastic plates. With thin scratches on the surface, as if the plate were fissured. As the plate is washed over and over, dirt gets lodged in the scratches, delineating spider-web like patterns. He takes the plate back to the aluminium-covered counter; the heavy, scowling old lady on the other side doesn't greet him. Relieved that this day too has passed, he walks along the main street of the little town towards the bus stop. The brightly shining sun on this early spring day makes him squint. At the intersection, where he has to turn off towards the bus station, is the decrepit Catholic church. Its doors are wide open, the vestibule closed off by a barred gate. The interior is oppressively threadbare, abandoned, the neglect visible on the crumbling plaster, the blistering frescoes, the pews in need of a fresh layer of paint. On the bus, he takes out the book he got from the library, looks at it. Something disturbs him, he closes it. The trip isn't long, he gets home quickly. What is missing from churches like that is space—they are all the same. Nothing disrupts that inner barren-ness they carry within themselves. They were built around the time of the First World War—before, after or even during the war. At first, such churches had no bell towers, then in time, often decades later, bell towers were added. The same design was often reused. There were never any intimate spaces, no leeway for the mystery of faith. By the end of the twentieth century, they had become completely deserted, the brick saltpetre walls gleaming white beneath the disintegrating plaster. Their doors yawning open, the musty damp smell dispersing over the sweaty and tired people hurrying towards the bus station: they were grateful for the cool relief of the breeze, but they turned up their noses, because the smell was unpleasant, evoking bad memories. The synagogue had been torn down long ago: the residents of the small town had dismantled it on that evening when the authorities looked the other way. The gendarmes hurried home, putting on their civilian clothes and rubbing smut on their faces so as not to be conspicuous among the throngs of plundering villagers. The hope of free goods had lured the entire town, the quickest to arrive were the gendarmes disguised as civilians: they recognized each other, but pretended not to. And that made everyone braver. Upstanding citizens, to begin with, watched from behind their shutters, then stood in the doorways. They shook their heads: this would lead to trouble. You couldn't just steal what someone else had earned over their entire life without consequences, they kept repeating, shaking their heads in evermore disbelief. Because neither the gendarmes nor the police showed up; no one from the military patrol was dispatched. Wives kept repeating: you go too, don't be a fool, you see it's permitted. So the respectable people got there too late: everything of value had been taken already, the cupboards pillaged, the flooring ripped out, the courtyards dug up, the dung heaps scattered as everyone searched for the hidden gold. Nothing designated where the Jewish district had once been, but the boy sensed it with certainty. He proceeded along the streets of what remained of it. He hurried to the bus stop.

In the enforced inactivity of the Sabbath, when it was forbidden to turn on a light and do any work, but reading was permitted, I picked up the book I'd borrowed from the district library the day before, the pages of which I'd began to turn over on the bus, to get to know this book, but as my eyes felt tired, I put it aside. In another book I'd read, someone had written that Kafka was the most decisive figure for him; I felt as if the writer could have been Kafka's brother, someone who knew everything about him. The foreword or afterword: at that time, it was customary to protect the unsuspecting reader through such statements, thus warning off anyone who might show any inclination for such bourgeois, decadent, Eastern European (for many: Jewish) literature. In the school I attended in those days, I was regarded with the same suspicion evinced by the forewords or afterwords of the books that I borrowed from the infrequently visited stacks of the district library due to the influence of precisely such suspicions. My glasses were strong, but I already needed a new pair, even stronger lenses. Short-sightedness protects one from the outer world; books, however, can provide a feeling of security. I withdrew to the large window, through which enough light still filtered, in the grey gloaming of morning, making it possible to read comfortably. So once again I took out Anselm Kafka's book, and, as if I'd gazed into a maelstrom, I fell into a sort of strange stupor. I saw all the fears and anxieties of my childhood take shape.

An Evening Stroll

We see Kafka step out the entrance of the apartment building known as 'Zum Schiff'. We are in the centre of Prague, in one of the newly rebuilt neighbourhoods, considered illustrious, close to the Moldau; where the well-to-do citizens of Prague live. In this part of the city, German is heard in the apartments, salons, and shops. But in the kitchens and servants' rooms and on the streets, one hears Czech mixed with Yiddish. Kafka stepped out of the building standing at the corners of Niklasstraße and XXX: it had many ground-level shops, and a few restaurants, among them the eatery known as 'Zum Schiff', also the name of the entire massive block; there was a tram stop in front. As Kafka exited the ornamented entranceway doors maintained for the residents and designed in a Secessionist spirit, a tram arrived. The brakes creaked. [The house] had been built on the corner of the demolished Prague ghetto according to philanthropic principles of modern urban planning. The city fathers dreamt of brand-new luxury buildings replacing unhealthy congestion; the builders saw the enterprise as excellent business. In the interests of the Empire, the Austrian-Hungarian monarchy, the *k. und k.*, the Imperial and Royal administration supported the City of Prague's plans for the ghetto's demolition and the building of a new and fashionable city quarter suited to the challenges of the present. The age was full of contradictions, unpredictable and decadent, just like the Emperor and the King, Franz Josef I, whom personal fate had rendered unhappy, although it could have hardly been otherwise, for there was a curse was upon him. As a young ruler—just acceded to the throne—he had been compelled to save the Empire by preventing the succession of Hungary, its largest province, to strengthen the foundations of the Empire by humiliating the Hungarians, handing down death sentences for thirteen military leaders of the War of Independence, among whom there were hardly any born Hungarians: most of them didn't even speak Hungarian, they were Austrians, who, characteristically for the Empire, hailed from many different ethnicities. All this happened a long time ago in 1849, when the Prime Minister, Lajos Batthányi, was sentenced to death, the young Franz Josef . . . : the executions were carried out in the courtyard of the barracks in Pest, by the southwestern wall of the Neugebäude; considering Batthányi's rank, however, he was not to be hanged—he came from one of the most ancient Hungarian noble families, often marrying into equally ancient Austrian families—but executed by firing squad.

Tradition has it that Batthányi, before his death, called attention to that heinous deed—previously inconceivable in both a political and moral sense, revealing the baseness of the young Emperor, who betrayed Hungary's legally elected prime minister, his own constant, unwavering adherent, a representative of the

aristocracy, betraying as well honour, birth-endowed trust in privilege, and the tranquillity assured by societal rank—Batthányi called attention to that deed by cursing the young king and emperor, still a child compared to him. According to tradition, there were very few who heard the curse that rang out in the closed courtyard of the Neugebäude, that curse which Count Batthányi, scion of an ancient family—producing many princes as well—pronounced in German (his mother tongue) but which was passed on in Hungarian: 'May Heaven and Hell destroy his happiness! May his dynasty vanish from the face of the earth! May he be smitten by God in the hearts of his loved ones! May his life be only ruin, may his children perish wretchedly!' Sixty-three years had passed since that curse, burdening the King and Emperor who was shattered when he saw it fulfilled; as a young man he too had heard it, but hadn't given it much thought, even forgetting it for a while, and now it was as if his long life only served for him to observe, to witness how his suffering could be drawn out even further as he witnessed the ruin of his family and his loved ones in addition to the ruin of his empire, and the most painful of all: the suicide of his son, Crown Prince Rudolf, who had ended his own life with one of his lovers, a woman below his rank, thus sending a message to his parents. Then the Emperor and King could observe his wife's existence, driven into insanity, her harshness and self-adulation, her self-accusations and escape into self-torture after her son's death until a lunatic anarchist stabbed her in the heart with a sharpened file, stabbing the Emperor's heart as well for eternity, the Emperor who still lived and functioned like a machine, but more like a marionette for whom everything is false. And Prague, the northern metropolis of the Empire, in this ruin-world, built on appearances, looked towards Vienna: it listened to the fragments of conversation floating out from the windows of the Burg, it listened to the breath of the King and Emperor starting awake every night, to his snoring, this or that longer silence giving rise to hope but then always disappointed because with a panicked intake of breath the body of the King and Emperor huffed and puffed onward, the moustache-trainer rigorously guarding his manly ornament, drops of sweat appearing on his bald skull, suddenly running down the liver spots, and the cumbersome body groaning while turning, the flatulence loudly exiting the body. But he was still alive—or so it seemed. Beneath the surface of the Empire, disintegration and ruin were already slowly charting their paths. The smell of cadavers spread throughout the Empire, Kafka's irritably sensitive nose wrinkled, responding to this horrific, enigmatic and yet sweetish smell.

* * *

So it was in the year 5672, on the last, 30th day of the month of Av, on 13 August 1912 according to the Christian calendar, a Tuesday, when Kafka, after his afternoon nap, went for a stroll in the coolness after a hot summer's day, walking from the banks of the Moldau and Rudolf Park, in the air made fragrant by the cool evening breezes along Hradschin. He was already past the trials of Monday, always the most difficult day for him to re-enter his workplace; in the evening, he went for a stroll. It was as if he'd spent the whole day in a dream, like Sleeping Beauty, the lassitude also occasioned by the overheated offices of the Workers' Accident Insurance Institute, as if it had never stopped being Sunday, when everyone, grown heavy from the midday meal, lay on divans in darkened sitting rooms, awaiting the relief promised by the setting sun, when they would set off for the evening promenade on Niklasstraße and the Großer Ring; there, on warm evenings, the vendors offering ice-cold drinks unpacked their wares: raspberry syrup, chilled apricot juice and lemonade pearled with beads of moisture, placed on straw between the ice blocks. But this evening turned out differently than was usually the case with Herr Doctor, as Kafka was addressed in his workplace; his friends also called him that, playfully and with a little fillip, just like his father who never forgot to slip a note of sarcasm into this salutation with its respectfulness nested within flattery. His stroll, with its circuitous diversions, led him in the direction of his dearest friend, Max Brod, but he was postponing his arrival, which anyone else might have taken as vulgar discourtesy; Kafka, though, had gained a particular acceptance from the Brods; for him, the day only really began during these hours, just as his life began with the lunar calendar's rise of the moon. Then later, leaving the Brods' flat, he accompanied, with Max, a woman back to her hotel—a woman who from this point on would play a determining role in Kafka's life, just as her figure may not be omitted from this book. Midnight was fast approaching, or perhaps it was past midnight, and perhaps it was already the first day of the month of Elul when the summer heat began to recede, and amid the laughter and mutual banter of the two friends, they accompanied the marriageable visitor from Berlin towards the newly built Prager Repräsentationshaus. The days were still too warm for the fall of dusk not to present a larger temptation to stroll for all those whose constitution and schedule permitted. Twilight refreshed Kafka's mood, he woke from the slumber of his new daily routine; at last he felt restored and refreshed. He sensed tonight he would write: his intuition told him that everything he would put to paper would be light and exciting.

Kafka and the Words

The evening stroll had not been a sudden idea, for they had spoken of it the day before; still, its realization combined many contingencies into this undertaking which might even look like an adventure. Perhaps it occurred that Anselm K. did not recall how he turned up in this city, seemingly built out of words. The streets had names, indicated on various kinds of enamel plaques, although some were already mottled with rust spots. He looked up at one, Ziegenhaufenstraße, finding its name, 'Goat-Heap Street', to be unusual. When he turned around again to look at this strange word, it now read: Ziegenstraußenstraße. He did not recall ever having heard of a plant called 'goat's bouquet' so he wanted to look at it one more time to make sure he hadn't been mistaken. This time, the name of the street was Ziegenleichenstraße, 'Goat Corpse Street': when he read it, he shuddered with dread, as he had pictured it in his mind immediately.

Already, the night before, Anselm K. had slept badly because he knew he had to meet his father. He did not like to meet his father. And it was as if this unpleasant feeling, one which he could never openly avow to himself, was shared by his father. His father was dead: this only increased the feeling of unpleasantness. Why doesn't he at least have a body? Anselm K. asked himself. Every proper father has one that he wears continuously, not just sometimes, like a winter coat, when fog covers Judengasse, a sharp wind blows from the Moldau, and everyone pulls their hats down over their eyes, grabbing their coats by the collar, hunching forward, almost as if lying down upon the harsh wind blowing at waist height. In the streets where the Orthodox Jews live, the black caftans float around the light, scrawny bodies as they too lean forward, nearly flying, trying to pull down their wide round-brimmed hats onto their heads, because what would the Almighty say if they were to stand there in the icy wind bareheaded, without their kippahs and marten-fur hats, like bald little sparrows tumbled out of the nest. Instead, they clutched onto their hats, prescribed to them by the Law, with all their might—the Law, the letter of which was more important than any storm or chill, more important than life itself. That is why these shades hovered in the turbulent wind slashing across Judengasse, their legs high above the pavement of the street, their caftans stretched around them like wings; like large and clumsy birds they fluttered from one wall to the next, the wind rolling them around as they clutched desperately at their hats forced down onto the crown of their heads, and their earlocks beat about, twisting next to their ears.

Poor Jews, Anselm thought, or perhaps grumbled, muttering to himself, you poor little idiot Jews, why don't you come down to earth, why not walk on your own two legs, why don't you understand that your caftans are only good for the wind to catch at them, then they roll you along like the burning breath of the desert rolling along the Rose of Jericho, this unassuming little skein, a dried-out bird's nest, and you stumble between the long panels of your caftans, clumsily thrashing like a crow trying to walk in the wind.

You're late again, said the father, who was standing in front of their apartment building waiting for Anselm, angrily shifting his weight from one foot to the other. It was inconceivable, on the night before Yom Kippur, for a father not to go to synagogue, even if he hadn't set foot there the entire year, to the rabbi's great sadness and disapprobation. But that is why it was precisely inconceivable for the head of the family, the father, not to go to synagogue on the eve of Yom Kippur, as he had hardly set foot in there all year long—only when, immersed in the details of a contract or agreement with some client, someone else took him there, and Hermann could only think about possibility of gain, all the work and energy he'd put into the deal, the client practically ready to sign. So he didn't mind and didn't pay much attention, let them go to synagogue if they were already here and that Grün, Gelb or Schwartz, or whoever also had to go to evening prayers tonight, he would go with them and not leave the matter half finished, otherwise tomorrow he'd have to start over and the expected advantage (which he wouldn't even necessarily call profit), wouldn't be enough to make it worthwhile to begin the whole process again. The hell with it, he'd recite the evening prayers with them, he'd been coming here for a long time anyway, the rabbi always receiving his greeting with a meaningful emphasis in his voice, and none of his relatives or kinfolk would set foot in

Hermann's business even by accident. So be it: the details could be discussed more thoroughly during prayers, and he'd give a big smile to the rabbi to show him that all the same he was a good Jew, even though, as it happened, he hadn't brought his tallit today, but of course he wasn't the only one who . . . this death shroud, supposed to be worn during prayer by every male head of the family. This always bothered Hermann, ever since his father had died, he did not think willingly about death, especially not the possibility of his own, and the tallit, which had to be worn underneath one's clothes, the tzitzits had dangling out nicely, signified this: the tallit would remain with him in the grave, he would be buried in it; its role was to remind him, ever since he'd got married and had children, that death now loomed closer than birth. And, as one who had gained continuation, from the grace of the Eternal, in the form of his children, he no longer need fear death, for the Almighty, blessed be His name, had saved him, with His grace, from final and irrevocable destruction. But this was of less interest to Hermann at the moment than his business, his stocks and his connections, which although difficult to enumerate, still represented significant material, if not to say, market values. These were the kinds of things, along with the consciousness of possessing them, that made Hermann happy, and not confronting the possibility of losing it all from one day to the next—not temporarily, so that with a lucky turn, or his own work or persistence, he could win it all back—but definitively and irrevocably. This 'definitively and irrevocably', like the closing clauses of a contract, always struck him as a kind of legalese, a lawyer's trick, empty and meaningless words, without which, however, the entire contract would be invalid, and therefore he also viewed them as a kind of ritual text: he shuddered at these words, because they were inconceivable to him.

That had been the last time he had gone to synagogue, and it remained a good memory, as the contract had been set up, yielding much more profit, later on, than Hermann had originally hoped for; as such, his visit to the synagogue appreciated in value in his eyes, and lately it even seemed as if there might be a kind of connection between prayer, the gaze of the Almighty, and the blessing, also interpretable as business profit. And that is why, as they stepped into the small prayer room of the Altneu Synagogue that evening, he began to look upon that God differently, his God and that of his fathers, the God of whom his goy business partners were jealous. But it was already autumn, the tenth day of the month of Tishri in the year 5672. And by that point many things had occurred, so let's not rush ahead too much.

Kafka at the Rabbi's

When Kafka grew tired and was lost among the words, he once went, in his desperation, to the rabbi; people were in the habit of asking the rabbi for help with their troublesome daily matters, so Kafka thought he could also help someone who was lost among the life-signifying words. We don't know exactly what the rabbi thought when this strange, lanky figure knocked at his door; he only recalled very vaguely that perhaps he'd seen him once before, perhaps in the synagogue on one of the High Holidays; when the lanky man introduced himself, he realized who he was at once, for everyone in the city knew the father, Hermann Kafka, especially in this part of town where Hermann's business was located. Kafka introduced himself as Anselm Kafka, using his Hebrew name, because he thought that was proper, and clearly that was what the others did. He felt he could not pronounce his civic name to the rabbi—a name recorded in the Imperial and Royal offices, signifying servility and alienation, formulated in the tongue of ignominy; a name which, if he thought about it more deeply (and apart from the Jewish hocus-pocus of everyone else also having a second name), had nothing to do with him at all. The name of Franz was just as alien and incomprehensible to him as the name of Isaac; it was as fearful as the name of Hermann.

Anselm Kafka did not know the Jews, even though he was always seeing a few of them on the street as they hurried somewhere, because they were always hurrying somewhere. Their black caftans flew after them, while their prayer shirts flashed white from below, their prayer shirts with those tassels whose purpose was entirely mysterious to Kafka. They wore hats, their ear locks hanging down. They were always debating, always talking about something. They were restless, dark figures. This was what people thought Jews were like, he knew. The rich Jew with his enormous paunch, the large jowls that trembled as he spoke. That already made them suspicious in his eyes. Because his father wasn't at all like them, and at home he was the one who cursed the Jews the most. Franz didn't understand why his father cursed the Jews, why he acted as if he wasn't one himself. The rabbi, on the other hand, undoubtedly looked like who he was. This instilled a feeling of trust in Kafka, who himself looked as if he did not resemble the person he was in reality.

I want to tell stories, Rabbi, I've realized that writing will only save me if I tell stories. For me, words can only have meaning if they can protect me from life, and they can only protect me from life if I am able to join them together as stories, moreover stories that make my own traces disappear, stories that will remain between the words in my wake. My pursuers, following scattered indications, will soon catch up with me, they plan to finish me off prematurely, but if I can make these traces disappear, stitching them into stories, then I have a chance of escape. I hope you understand me. You do understand, don't you? Kafka implored the rabbi. Surely you must understand. The problem is I don't know how to tell stories. The world is full of stories that don't speak to me. There's hardly even one worth reading. Perhaps some of Flaubert's—if you know who I'm talking about. I know, the Torah is full of stories. But those are the stories of God, and it just so happens that I can't find God anywhere. This is why I need to tell stories, so I can find Him. And as I don't know how to tell stories, I can't find anyone anywhere to whom I could tell those stories that are my own.

They stood in the inner courtyard of the synagogue: it was summer, the afternoon sun shone down upon them, it was the third of July, a Tuesday, the walls had been absorbing the summer heat for days, the paving stones radiated heat, the fragrance of the lavender planted next to the wall was soothing to Franz, slowly he slipped into the consciousness that everything surrounding them was mere illusion, everything was but mere appearance, false and perfidious. What was happening here could happen anywhere and at any time, and perhaps it was all happening somewhere else and at another time, there was nothing new here—merely two Jews having a conversation, one was lost and sought guidance from the other, who, however, was troubled by this trust, for he sensed that responsibility which he could sense anywhere and at any time. The rabbi perhaps knew, perhaps felt everything which Franz was thinking about much more precisely, he measured this man's [ ]

You must tell the story in such a way that you will be helping people in the telling, the rabbi replied, scrutinizing Kafka's face at length before he spoke. He was not searching for the features of Hermann whom he had just now recollected, but for that moment in the past when they might have met up in Jerusalem: decades ago, millennia ago, perhaps in Toledo, or somewhere by the Rhine. The rabbi concentrated all his strength on this face, because the fear he saw on Franz's features was much deeper, pointing to something much more distant than that fear with which the Prague Jews knocked at his door. The dread he saw on Kafka's face was familiar to him, the uncertainty accumulated over millennia; the rabbi carried it in his own soul as well.

We have lost most of the writings. We have lost the words that were written down, not to mention the words that were never written down. So much loss, if you think about it, young man, my dear Albert Kafka.

Anselm, Kafka immediately corrected him.

Forgive me, Anselm. In other words, think about how there is nothing in comparison to what we have already lost. Everything we possess can only be perceived in the light of this immeasurable loss. And if we look at things from this perspective, then our situation does seem to be rather desperate, giving us cause for not even the most trifling of good spirits. And yet, despite all this— as you yourself know more than anyone else—despite all this we must have hope, for you wouldn't be standing here now if you didn't have hope in at least some kind of answer from me, for in the end we are the people of hope, my dear Adolf . . .

Anselm, Kafka once again hastened to correct the distinguished rabbi.

Anselm, to hell with it, I keep mixing up your name, Herr Kafka. You know, Herr Kafka, your question has completely thrown me off balance. No one has ever asked me anything like this before.

You know—the rabbi continued—I've been waiting my entire life to be able to say to someone that hope is something like our ability to forget. Both are enormous and difficult forms of knowledge, granted to us, to the Jews, least of all. Particularly forgetting. Never forget that. Although I can see by your face that there is no need for me to enjoin you. Write it all down, I ask you, always write it down. Then, straining with your entire soul, read it over again and again and try to grasp the meaning. This is what our teachers did for millennia. Nothing remains from their notations, and from your own very little will remain, but perhaps even so it will be too much to disturb people, and yet undisputedly too little to give them something to hang onto. Every piece of writing leads to the void, never forget that. Although, as I've mentioned, you are the last person I have to explain this to. And if I may, please pass on my greetings to your father. I would be very happy to see you both in synagogue on the Sabbath. The son follows in the father's footsteps. Shalom, said the rabbi, and he had already turned away, departing with hurried steps like someone who was late and would have to compensate for his absence.

Kafka Writes

We see Kafka at dawn, perhaps at around 4 a.m. because the sun has not yet risen, although the lower edge of the sky already gleams with a pale light; Kafka leans over the desk and writes quickly, he's hurrying. He didn't sleep this past night, he found his rhythm. He's been working for days now on a story, but had to break off writing several times. A trip he was obliged to make, to Leitmeritz, was particularly unpleasant. He was selected from his workplace to represent the Insurance Company, far away from Prague, in a completely insignificant matter, one in which he would clearly commit no errors. But it was a completely senseless journey, because the negotiations ended up being postponed, although he was not informed of this lamentable error in time. The trip turned Kafka's work schedule upside down.

But, at last, he could sit down again at his desk, try to return to the state in which he'd begun writing. For Franz, the story he is writing can never be predicted. He never knows where it will lead, only senses it obscurely. That is why every time he writes, he feels utterly defenceless. He himself watches, agitated, to see what will happen to his characters. At times they reproach him—why doesn't he help? The only thing that Franz can do is to try to depict them. He draws them as they are. They're made of ink, mere sketches, like stick figures. They have no faces: he would have to know much more about them for that. They are dark figures, woven from the letters' dense web, their forms granted by the white spots remaining on the ink's confluent surface. Franz is afraid of these figures: still, he observes them, fascinated, but aware he must be on guard, for he knows they're watching him too; some of them, the more depraved ones, could attack him at any time. It is with this agitation that Franz opens his notebook, to continue the story he had to put aside. In his hand is a fountain pen, the cap carefully unscrewed and placed before him. This diminutive instrument with its steel needlepoint is also a tool of self-defence: if by any chance one of these small figures were, in its bitterness, to attack him, he could easily stab it. He therefore keeps the implement, something like a steel lance, close at hand as he opens the notebook, so that, if necessary, he can, with that spear clutched in his fingers, protruding from his fist—like a smaller version of St George—stab any one of these deprived figures. It is crucial that the fountain pen be of the best quality. Franz picks out these tools, which will also serve to protect him, if necessary. He can gauge how much ink is left in the cartridge by looking through the tiny glass window. He observes the small air bubbles moving around in the cartridge, sees pictures in the azure-coloured liquid. He always uses the same brand of ink. He uses a specific pen for writing, superstitiously believing that he can write stories with only that. He also has a special pen for writing novels. But when he writes to Felice, he uses a different pen altogether, reserved exclusively for this purpose. He has a particular connection to it. Felice touched this pen when, on the thirteenth of August, in Max Brod's apartment, Kafka reached across the table to show Felice some photographs. Franz's desk lamp casts a pale yellow circle of light onto the paper and onto his desk, overlaid with cherrywood veneer. On the photographs, black and white areas alternated with each other, in certain sections the surface of the paper gleamed. The matt surface of the photographs made everything seem duller, the sea reminiscent of the colour of cappuccino, the trees' green foliage like silhouette cut-outs, and, due to the lack of colour one could not decide if the women were wearing morning or afternoon visiting hats, otherwise one would know at what hour the photograph had been taken. In some areas, the darker spots had faded to a coffee-like hue: in time, they would fade completely. Across the entire surface of the photograph, the emulsion was beginning to crack, turning brown and resembling, more than anything else, a sheet of paper smeared with faeces. A photograph could never be developed without some flaw. A written description, on the other hand, was not endangered by these chemical processes, as long as the ink did not fade completely. That is why Franz always insisted on the best quality, no matter what it might be. In the end, he spent money on few things. He could permit himself that, even if the Insurance Company paid him little, thus, as his Papa used to say, obliging his own son to sponge off of him.

Just as in the office, Franz pulls on a felt cuff to protect the sleeve of the one single jacket that he always wears from the ink dripping onto the paper, the blots that can get carelessly smudged in the impetus of writing. Franz likes to write quickly. He likes it when the story is born from momentum, if possible one single momentum. Each hesitation feels like a betrayal to him. Because this is a question of his life—he senses that with evermore certainty. He has never seen the situation so clearly as he does now: for him, there are no other open paths, that is why all his ambitions are concentrated on this, all his strength is kept in reserve for when he sits down at the writing desk. He sees himself as nothing more than an instrument in the service of writing: his entire being is nothing more than waiting, expectant readiness. He has enlisted himself in the service of a power much greater than he, unknown to him and suspected only dimly, but if it does exist, then he is in its service. And so, if this higher power does exist, this power that wants to use him, and perhaps it is using him, then he curls up in its palm as one of its finely wrought instruments; because if it does not exist, then I am nothing, he says, and I simply remain here alone in frightening emptiness.

Writing is a futile goal, however, if there is nothing to transform it into renunciation—and not a purpose unto itself. He was close to thirty when he realized that he would only be able to annihilate that purpose, continually retreating before him, if he could place it in correlation to something else. Writing loses sight of its assigned goal only if, while writing, he recalls that he is supposed to be somewhere else; time devoted to writing is time stolen from another. If, through writing, he withdraws from something, as, for example, from his workplace, that is impersonal and therefore not sufficiently effective; even more so, if he withdraws from another person. This sacrifice only becomes discernible for him if the one from whom he withdraws sees his writing as inconsequential, meaningless; accordingly, they will not sense the loss being done them, the competition that should make them jealous. His ideas leave Felice cold; for her, his passion for writing is inconceivable, and Franz's renouncement is only comprehensible in that it means certain inevitable obstacles on the path towards the level-headed and palpable goals of family and children. Felice has her seemingly self-denying work at the offices of Lingenström & Co. as a way of expressing the pain caused by her mother—although her work seems more like self-withdrawal to Franz—so none of this is so terribly urgent. It means that Franz has time to convince Felice of what is most important for him, this question of life and death—as he knows with ever-increasing certainty—writing itself. His father disapproved of how Franz spent his days writing, as if he were still a pupil even in adulthood, a pupil whose ear might be grabbed by the teacher at any moment and made to kneel on the maize kernels before being quizzed about his homework, and if he didn't know the answer, he would remain there, to his shame. His father remembered those days when he had been humiliated in school, when he could hardly wait to leave, just as he wished to forget his own father as quickly as possible, his father who sat around in his butcher's shop among the many pieces of dead animals, his countenance gloomy, muttering prayers amid the putrid stench of red meats, the tzitzit, the prayer shawl, gathered up in his hands, rubbing its tassels between his fingers, and he awaited only one thing: for the evening prayers and the arrival of the Sabbath bride, when, as he stepped into the synagogue, he could once again feel he was a free man. For him, the synagogue meant freedom from the land of slavery. The children starving at home, the mother with her haggard face, Hermann shivering in his worn-out shoes, Hermann, who had to freeze in order to augment the family income, supplementing his mother's household money by working for the rabbi so the siblings wouldn't starve, so there could be some meat on the Sabbath table, so his father would have wine for the kiddush, for without that, a Sabbath table wasn't worth much. But in vain was the Sabbath table so beautiful, in vain did the candle, sliced into pieces and purchased on credit, shine in the battered pewter candleholder, in vain was the roast chicken fragrant, the polished pewter goblet filled to the brim with wine for the blessing, if it made one only temporarily forget that fervour for the Scriptures did not bring happiness, even Hermann's father said so. Hermann could never forgive his father's neglect, his mother's tears, the quiet patience she forced upon herself out of piety, but which undermined any resistance she might have summoned, the love of her children too little to save her from her early death which Hermann never accepted or exonerated in his father. The judgement that he passed was, therefore, to exile himself, far away; he would never have anything to do with all those Jewish things his father couldn't escape until his death, even though he could have been an outstanding merchant. Hermann wanted his son to follow in his footsteps. Franz, however, never showed any interest towards the shop. He often accompanied his father when he walked back to the shop after the afternoon nap; Franz, who suffered from insomnia, had been locked in his room by the maid, so that, like everyone else, he could take his rest, but then the father freed him, saying the child will come with me, he's not sleeping anyway. Franz was especially grateful at times like this, he admired his gigantic papa who greeted everyone in a loud voice when he met them in the stairwell or on the street, and once he stepped into the shop, everyone sought his favour. Trading was in Hermann's blood, or at least that is how Franz imagined it, he didn't have to study anything, he knew somehow in advance how to get people to buy something they didn't need through flattery and endearments, appealing to their vanity or their desire for profit. Hermann's virility, which made men uncertain and wrapped women around his little finger, was a part of the business. Franz saw how his father showered attention on the more well-to-do seeming customers. He saw it, and he found it repugnant. His father, at those times, seemed unmanly. He knew well that the roles between men and women could shift. There are men who, in face of another man, play the role of a woman. It seemed at those times that his father emasculated himself in the hopes of a good deal. Franz knew that as soon as a given customer stepped into the shop, Hermann had already decided how to deal with them. He sensed how much money the person was going to spend in his establishment. Of course, that wasn't the amount they were *intending* to spend; on the contrary, he explained to Franz, when he was in a good mood, feeling more communicative, or in the genial undulating momentum after a sale that surpassed his own expectations. The true task, you know, my son, the true task of a salesman is to know how much he can pull out of a customer's pocket, even though the customer has no intention of spending that much money. Most likely he didn't even want anything, he just stepped into the shop out of boredom, led by habit, and against his better judgement. And he himself doesn't understand, as he leaves and he thinks back onto that stupefaction, the vortex he fell into, he thinks to himself: did I really need to buy those lace underwear when they're not even my wife's size, I'm certainly not going to wear them, even though they're made of such fine material. Or the lady will think, as she heads homeward, what will my husband say, why did I let myself be talked into buying that moustache trainer, my husband doesn't even have a moustache, only the neighbours' lad.

But I can get at least twenty crowns out of this one. Just watch and see how I do it, Hermann said, and with a subservient smile hurried to the ladies in whom there was a mixture of provocation and impudence. These bored bourgeois women liked seeing the flirtatious papa; the men liked the self-debasing rival, the witty conversationalist who flattered the femininity or masculinity of their interlocutors, even if they knew it was only a game, that they were being wooed only in the hope of profit; this flirtation would not produce the slightest of infidelities. Even temptation was false.

Franz had no wish to go into trade: the insurance office contained, within itself, a clearer definition of roles, even if it demanded no smaller degree of dissimulation and playacting. Kafka quickly determined that writing would save him from everything with which his papa, through his life, had not been able to cope, and while Hermann was so proud of everything he

44

had achieved, as he put it, alone, with no help from anyone else, Franz sensed—knew with evermore clarity—that it was writing that would save him from being like his papa whom he pitied for his entire wasted life. For the blindness with which the gods had smote him. In place of his papa's steel-grey, flashing gaze, Franz saw two bloody cavities from which purulent liquid dripped onto his elegant, carefully knotted tie, which, however, was always knotted by his mama, because Hermann never learnt how to properly knot or wear a tie—an unnecessary and foolish item of clothing, in his view. Jews don't wear ties, what is this anyway, what needless ostentation. All these ties are good for is stringing up Jews when the next pogrom comes. Or they can string themselves up, he muttered at length, grumbling and vexing everyone, if, before a family gathering, he once again compromised and had Julie knot his tie. But then he got used to wearing them, moreover he even judged ties as mandatory for his work, and in that way also exempted himself from obligatory shame when he opened up his haberdashers, for items such as ties specifically brought in the greatest profit: it was fitting for him to appear in the shop wearing the most fashionable cravats.

Writing was the purest of activities in which a person could engage to free himself from his own weight, a weight pressing down upon him so heavily that, with the passage of time, it would bury him completely. His own errors, his own deficient self-image bound him hand and foot evermore, every word he ever uttered, every word that ever escaped from his mouth weighting him down like lead weights: he was beginning to collapse underneath this burden that was the luxury of his life, Kafka noted, full of those doubts and lies with which one generation is replaced by the next, unsuspecting. With what a dry mouth do I wait every evening beside my writing table, bereft of hope before the blinding desert of pure white paper where I must close my eyes so that nothing of this radiance will blind me, and how does my pen drag itself, in my convulsively crooked hand, every evening wandering off in vain to the banks of the River Lethe, so that the yearning that arises in me every time I write might be extinguished, after the loss of memory.

Kafka and the Letters

One time a pious merchant returned from the market, but you know that he'd got a little tipsy the day before. He was pleased with the good business which turned out better than he'd hoped. You know, the poor man who always just loses, and loses in business, he gets used to the idea that he can never win. He only adds up the losses: no toys for the children, no presents, once again he'll have to listen to the wife's grousing. He adds these things up when he must—all the small losses set against his trifling income—and again renounces the idea of coming out ahead in a trade. He whose pocket is empty must take the offer he is given; if not, he can wait until the arrival of the Messiah for the next one. But by the time the Messiah comes, the rich will have made their advantageous deals at the expense of the poor. In brief, as you know, when a poor man is happy, even his joy cannot be unclouded. That's how things were for our merchant as well: and, because this time business had been somewhat less bad, well, and because of the bad conscience that had been accumulating in him during the Days of Repentance, he recited the blessing many times over for the One who gave us wine, and who did not spare us good kosher schnapps as well, blessed be His name, and, as punishment for this, he set off on his journey home later than planned. Punishment did not delay in coming, namely, the load atop the battered cart—which looked light but was still too heavy—broke the side of the cart. It tilted, toppling over; well, so he had to repair it, taking his bundles down and loading everything up again. And time passed: when he continued his journey, the sun was hurrying to set behind the clouded autumnal sky already growing dark. The pious man regretted his sin, but there was nothing to be done, he was forced to perceive that his shame was futile, it would be even a greater sin to break the High Holiday than to remain distant from the congregation, gathered in the synagogue on Yom Kippur. When he saw the abandoned stables next to the road, he turned in that direction, having decided that no matter how sad it was to spend the holiday alone, he had no choice, and even more so because, in this way, by the time he got back, his wife wouldn't be able to tell he'd been badly hung over. Assuming that his name would be written down in the book of life. He didn't think too much about this, although a fearful thought came to mind: because that book, in which the bustling servants of the Almighty, blessed be His name, wrote down the names of all the mortals—strictly according to their merits, of course—was, for him, the most fearsome secret. The secret of secrets.

Journey to Leitmeritz

That morning, K. got up earlier than usual. For the most part, he was a bad sleeper. His new schedule, allowing him to resolve his stomach complaints as well as his issues with writing, still wasn't fully operational, with occasional disruptions of workplace or family expectations. He slept little and restlessly, following different rhythms than others. But now he was much more restless than usual. He didn't like—indeed, he hated—travelling, always postponing it if he could.

For him, the noise and commotion, the people pushing and shoving, were unbearable. He wasn't happy to talk with anyone, because every conversation only swept him farther away from the goal he'd set for himself of arriving at his destination as early as possible, thus preserving the unity of the journey. If he was forced to speak with someone, he suddenly felt as if he were leaving his body; he watched this gangling figure from outside. And he immediately sensed he hadn't been able to say what he wanted to. There was also some kind of coat hanging off his shoulders, which wouldn't have been so objectionable if he didn't look such an idiot in it. The hat perched on his head was no more reassuring. Lurking behind this bohemian exterior was a pitiful longing to be equal to the occasion, causing the scene to lose all its charm and artlessness.

These forced conversations, usually taking place in such locations as a railway carriage, left Kafka thoroughly confused. The doubling caused in him by travel, a state in which he simultaneously saw himself from outside and from above, as well as within any given situation, was as if body and soul, as people termed it, had become detached from each other. Kafka also suffered from this doubling in a general sense, because his life made him feel as if he were not only present within every moment but standing outside of it as well. Now, once again, because of travel, his fears returned, because he saw himself from outside.

* * *

Kafka stepped out of the building known as 'Zum Schiff', on the corner of Niklasstraße and Josephsplatz. To the right, an empty lot—the edge of the demolished ghetto—gaped amid the buildings. Kafka had recently become interested in these Jewish things of which his father spoke with only contempt and disparagement. The Jews believe in superstition, the Galician Jews are the most dangerous, the Hasidim keep on living in their ghettos, ghettos they build themselves from words, old wives' tales and superstitions. Jews like that you can never take out of the ghetto. I'm telling you, the father said, they will, with all their devotion, insist on having a new ghetto built for themselves where the other Jews will leave them alone with their foolishness. For it is written:

Cursed is he who trusts in people; they should know, however, that there are neither miracles nor miracle workers. There are only conjurers and the gullible. The wind brought the scent of the River Moldau from the direction of the Čech Bridge. At times like this, the trams aren't running yet. Kafka adjusts the fashionable small top hat which he had bought for the journey, he usually doesn't wear such hats. To handle this business matter, he needs to look more serious than he usually does here in Prague. The interests of the Institute are his interests as well, although he could send this trip to the devil. The dawn mist glistened on the cobblestones. Sometimes, Kafka slipped. He anxiously checked his own wristwatch against the church tower clock, but there was only a slight difference: one was a wristwatch, the other was a church tower clock, as he determined, but the time wasn't correct, he wasn't going to make a fuss about it, because he was already used to such things.

Passing in front of storefronts, Kafka saw his twin, moving beside him in the glass. He watched as the tall, almost ridiculously lanky figure glided next to him. From time to time the figure disappeared, then in the fogged glass of the next storefront it was visible again. When Kafka stopped in order to thoroughly scrutinize this figure reflected in the glass, his twin also came to a stop, turning towards him hesitantly. His coat, a men's overcoat of average length, the kind worn in the autumn, looked ridiculous on him. Beneath it, his legs dangled down like two lengths of packing rope, and as he walked, but especially when he was hurrying, his upper body leaning forward, the coat swayed and fluttered in the wind like an upside-down lampshade, or even more like a ringing bell, the packing-rope-like legs almost getting entangled in each other. Now Kafka saw the strange, irregular outlines of his twin's impeccably ironed trouser legs, drawn with India ink, fracturing at the interstice of the two panes of glass. In one spot, a length of about ten centimetres was missing, then it continued below. Kafka found this to be peculiar.

But then his attention was drawn by something completely different. He noticed two figures following him: they looked like strange operatives. One of them, vehemently conferring with the other, pulled a wide-bladed kitchen knife from his inside pocket. The other gesticulated in protest, upon which the first quickly hid the knife in his inner jacket pocket: an unusual place to store such an object. This was surprising behaviour, particularly for two such agents, as they appeared to be. Kafka soon put it out of his mind, though; he tried to convince himself that he'd been mistaken or otherwise was imagining things. Previously, passing in front of an entranceway, Kafka had peeked in and saw a corpse sitting upright in a recess in the wall. The bloody vomit gushing from his mouth, the body's unusual rigidity and the eye's fixed stare all bore witness to what could be determined from a distance as well. Kafka found it natural that a body bearing such symptoms and signs would be a corpse; he had no desire to approach or examine the matter more thoroughly. He had learnt in the office quickly enough that one could never approach one's caseload with either passion or interest, especially when outside one's sphere of responsibility. He conducted himself in accordance with this precept now as well, preferring to quicken his steps and move on. His suspicion that those two men were not following him accidentally but purposely, on some kind of assignment, was strengthened. He had to get to the train station—then he would be saved, he thought, because in the station there were so many people milling about both night and day, they couldn't really do anything to him. Kafka tried to shake off his pursuers by gliding into the entranceway of a nearby building: he opened the door, but before closing it, quickly wiped away the door handle, as if it were nothing more than a drawing, with his monogrammed handkerchief. From the other side of the door, he hears—through the keyhole which was not wiped away—his pursuers, he listens to their conversation; when he reaches the train station, the two men are waiting by the entrance, they greet him discreetly, then they get lost in the crowd, hiding the fact that they're still following him. But when Kafka steps into his train compartment, he glances back and sees the two men also getting onto the train. They, however, are travelling in Second Class. It reassures him that there is a difference between them, if in nothing else than the level of their pay grades.

My dear son,

I hope that my letter finds you in good health, that you are eating proper food, not only vegetables more suited for rabbits. Forgive me for bringing it up again, but I am a simple village Jew who is happy to see roast goose on the table for Shabbos because all week long he was starving. When my father opened his butcher's shop, the nicely smoked goose legs hung there in vain, in vain was there duck on the countertop, we couldn't eat any of it because we had to pay the rent, as well as the loan my father had taken out when he started the business. For years we children just looked at our papa with longing, as he stood there in his wonderful hat in the shop, the tzitzis of his prayer shawl peeking out from beneath his black caftan and the white apron hanging from his neck, because in those days a butcher was expected to dress in white, even if he was a Jew. We celebrated the Sabbath with leftovers: papa brought home the scraps he'd sliced off so the cuts of meat would look nicer. He was a kosher butcher, but the goyim also bought from him, because he always weighed everything accurately and never allowed unhealthy animals into his shop. Papa began the day in the synagogue, then he opened up the shop, but he could hardly wait for evening prayers. He never accepted anything more than the actual price. Never allowed himself to be tempted by anything. Otherwise—but I have said this many times already—he was as tall and thin as you, and when I think back on it, he also didn't eat meat. A man is not weak, he always said, but I saw that he wept when the young calves were slammed in the head with the shochet's hammer, the neck immediately sliced so the blood could spill out. The shochet's hands were bloody, and blood splashed onto his face, but he was quick, and the animal felt no pain, it was dazed from the blow and the knife of the angel of death reached it in that strange dream-like fainting. My father pronounced the blessing above the animal with the shochet—Papa was truly in his element then. But he wept when the blood flowed down into the trough. He waited with the shochet for the redness that carried life to flow out of the body, they tied slipknots around the animal's legs and lifted it with a hoist to help things along. My father's eyes were filled with tears; he didn't look at the shochet who knew that Papa was crying. Then he gave teachings to the shochet, who was happy to take part in this ritual because Papa liked most of all to think about the Talmud, this cheered him up and diverted his thoughts. The shochet asked Papa questions and drank up his words while the earth and the sewage disposal trough drank up the calf's blood. Papa lived in writing; he was hardly touched by anything else. As he was explaining scriptures to the shochet, the animal was being disassembled, its guts examined to make sure there were no defects. If everything was fine with the animal, then Papa prepared the separate cuts of meat for sale. He did all of this for his family, in his village a butcher's seemed like a good business, and it wasn't a bad idea. Gradually the business began to take off, the customers respected Papa, and the family was granted a certain subsistence. Papa was able to spend more time in the synagogue, he couldn't read in the butcher's shop anyway; if, though, there were no goyim in the shop, but only his fellow Jews, he continued the pilpul.

I don't even know why I'm telling you all of this. Perhaps so that you'll know that your grandfather, as a pious Jew, did eat kosher meat, albeit not very often, and that it isn't a sin. For him, the shop was a prison, he stayed there during opening hours, then went straight to the synagogue. He could have been a successful shop-keeper if he had wanted more, if he'd been a little more clever, if he hadn't insisted on keeping the prices low for so many years—inflation meant there was hardly any profit—in vain did my mother tell him: You must raise your prices, no one can expect you to be losing money. You're spending more to buy the animals then you make in selling them. But my father resisted for years, saying it was impossible: how could he sell meat to that poor Mrs Friedman for more money: she had eight children to raise, she couldn't pay, and it was evermore of a burden, the adolescents eating so much that it was impossible to feed them enough. But your children want to eat more as well, look at Hermann here, he's as tall as you but already twice as brawny as you are, I can't starve him. But papa held out for years, until finally he had to start buying on credit: he tried to keep it a secret from my mother, but when she found out, he finally raised his prices. Some of the more decent customers paid the difference to my mother, so their business wouldn't go bankrupt. I didn't want to be that kind of merchant. My mother told me it would be better if I didn't read the Torah, because it made my father crazy. A merchant shouldn't be a scholar. That's something for the rabbis. And I think that is very correct. That's something I can also say to you. But you too did not become a merchant; this somehow reassures me, though, I who am threatened by death every day, and then what will become of your mother and your poor sisters? That's why I decided you should work as a civil servant who never risks anything, never has to decide what to sell and for how much, and who—if he is industrious and honourable in his work—can perhaps sustain his family. At the Insurance Company, you are in the best place of all: make sure you keep your job, because one day, when I won't be here any more, you'll be able to stand on your own two feet.

Because all the same I'm a bad Jew, but it was my father's dreadful example that made me so; still, I've read enough of the Scriptures to know that Abraham wasn't such a wonderful father. In those days, everything was so different, and if the situation called for it, fathers could even sell their children. As for what you wrote me, even though a month has gone by already, I still can't get over how you make me responsible for everything. This fills me with pain: I have to finish my letter, because I feel my heart can't take it any more.

Kafka at the Window

We see Kafka waking up in the new luxury apartment building, 'Zum Schiff', recently constructed as one of the ornaments of Prague, located between the Old City and Josefsstadt on the edge of the old ghetto, at the end of Niklasstraße, connecting Old Town Square with the Čech Bridge, just then being constructed, before the street leads onto the bridge. The disorder on the square in front of the bridgehead, as well as the empty lot, helped in surveying the scene. The light of the wonderful deep-blue sky of August gleamed above the lazily undulating Moldau, and on the opposite bank, above the park named for Crown Prince Rudolf and the winding paths of the Belvedere. Kafka liked, after waking, if he had already lazed enough in bed, to look out the window. The window frame, from where he could follow life outside as an observer, was particularly dear to him. He had been especially pleased when his father announced that they would be moving from the house 'Zu den drei Königen' where they had rented an apartment on the second floor, to this new luxury building just then being built. Thanks to Papa's good fortune in business, they could move to a larger apartment on the fourth floor of the sumptuous building designed in Art Nouveau style. Franz's room was also more spacious here than it had been on Zeltnergasse. He had liked to watch street life from the window of their old apartment too: the dry-goods shop across the street, the shop girls standing outside waiting for customers, the customers as they entered the shop, then departing with the customary phrases; he could see his papa hurrying away in the morning, then coming home at lunchtime. After the lunchtime nap, he saw Hermann Kafka returning to his place of business, wearier now, whistling to himself in the motionless heat of midday. He saw the hansom cabs with their passengers, people strolling in the evenings as the dry heat of daytime abated.

He had a much better view from the fourth floor, he could see far into the distance: apart from a section of the sky, he could see the hill on the other bank of the Moldau, the tiny specks moving around in the park named for Crown Prince Rudolf, people strolling on a Sunday afternoon, the vapour of the steamboats continually going up and down the river, the boiling steam they emitted as the ship's horn blew, creating the sharp whistling sound, thus signalling to oncoming barges, another steamboat, or in greeting to the strollers on the riverbank. From his room, Kafka [. . .] the empty lot in front of the apartment building, Josephsplatz [ ]

The bridge was officially opened one year after Kafka's family had moved from Zeltnergasse. By then, they had grown used to living on the edge of the city, to the strange noises which were, luckily, less audible on the fourth floor. The ongoing construction, though, disturbed them for a long time. In the afternoons, Franz's delicate ears could hardly withstand the commotion. He was so exhausted from his workplace that, once home, he had to sleep after lunch. These afternoon naps gradually grew longer. When the bridge was opened for traffic in 1908, a multitude of Prague's curious residents marched over to witness the illustrious event where one could count on a glimpse of the dignitaries of the Empire, the Czech government and the church; after the public celebrations, the area around Josephsplatz emptied and the peaceful rhythms of wealthy city centre life resumed once again. Wagons hauled goods across the bridge in the evenings or in the early dawn hours. The nearby shops and taverns handled their affairs with discretion. The arc lamps glowed after the fall of dusk, and after their evening meal, the well-fed citizenry, battling their stomachs' disquiet, strolled back and forth. It was only on Sunday afternoons that life on the bridge sparkled, when the servant girls, employed by bourgeois families, had the day off; they strolled along the bridge, eyes meekly lowered as they observed the soldiers and apprentices on leave, who themselves were sizing up the girls with the intention of flirting, a brief adventure or marriage.

Franz, though, slept through the afternoon. The weekdays were filled with the tribulations of the office. These were endurable only with great difficulty, then, after his seventh year at work, his stomach gave up the ghost, somehow in parallel to the completion of his official duties. He did not take the various powders recommended by the famous specialists, each one accompanied by a thicket of specifications determining which one to be taken, when and how. This was all nothing but hocus-pocus, thought Kafka, and he didn't believe in it. The fashionable sanatoria didn't help either—the sanatoria visited by the bourgeois in ever-greater numbers in recent years, particularly by women, the evermore solitary wives, who, if their children were already at boarding school, as was increasingly the custom among aspiring upper-class families, were left with nothing and no tasks to complete apart from issuing commands to a few maids and servants. The smaller children were looked after by the dry- and wet nurses, the mother and her husband lived society life every evening, in the morning she was tired, at lunchtime she worried about the serving of lunch, after coffee and siesta, indispensable for one's health, she supervised the kitchen and the cook, looked over the larder and settled the kitchen budget. The years went by and there was nothing else, only the sanatorium, where the husband could not accompany her because of the shop, the factory, the office and other preoccupations. It was as if the sanatorium were a luxury prison, those gathered there held captive in the well-appointed surroundings because they didn't know how to deal with the world. And they could not escape, they didn't have the strength, their imaginations didn't allow it.

In this way, my late appearance—for nine o'clock had passed already—did not bode well. The two guests clashed in the family's minds: you, for whom they wished only everything that was good and beautiful, and myself, the professional destroyer of sleep, and so for your sake the piano was played, and for mine, for example, Otto kept skirmishing with the fire screen, as was his habit: that's how he always conveyed to me that it was time to go to sleep, and if one didn't know, he watched with incomprehension and annoyance. I however, had not even the slightest notion that I would be meeting a guest in the family, I had simply agreed with Max that I would meet with him at around 8 p.m. (and, as is my wont, I arrived an hour late) to discuss the order of my manuscripts with which I hadn't bothered in the slightest, although they had to be submitted the next morning. Why deny it, I was vexed to see there was a guest in the house. On the other hand, things were such that I was not in the least taken aback by this guest. I extended my hand across the large table, not even waiting to be introduced, you had just begun to rise from your seated position, and you gave me your hand with visible reluctance. I gazed at you fleetingly, sat down and sensed that everything was in the greatest order; I felt, in your presence, that gentle sense of encouragement which strangers, encountered in familiar circles, always produced in me. As I abandoned the idea of looking over the manuscript with Max, viewing the Thalia photographs proved an endearing diversion. (And for this turn of phrase, which precisely expresses my feelings at that moment, today, now that I am so far away from you, I could slap myself in the face.) You looked at the photographs very attentively, only glancing upward if Otto explained something, or if I handed you a new photograph. One of us, I no longer know who, commented on one of the pictures, resulting in a droll misinterpretation. For the sake of the pictures,

you even stopped eating, and when Max mentioned it, you replied
that there was nothing you hated as much as someone who eats
all the time. Then the doorbell rang (it is already late now, 11
o'clock in the evening, when I usually begin my work, but I cannot
get away from this letter), accordingly, the doorbell rang, you,
right at that moment were describing the opening scene of the
operetta *The Autogirl* which you had seen in the Residenz Theatre
(is there a theatre with that name? And was this an operetta?),
fifteen performers stood on the stage, and from the antechamber,
where the sound of a ringing telephone came, somebody entered,
and walking over in turn to each actor, called each one to the telephone with the same phrase. I recall the phrase even today, but
I'm ashamed to note it down, because I don't know how to
pronounce it correctly or even how to write it, well, although that
only did I hear it precisely, but I also read it from your lips, since
then it has turned round in my head countless times, always, in
the struggle for the correct formulation. Then (but not earlier,
because I was sitting by the door, across from you diagonally), I
don't know how, but the conversation turned to the topic of
beatings and siblings. The names of certain family members were
uttered, ones I'd never heard before, I recall the name of Fény
(perhaps your older brother?), and you mentioned that when you
were a little girl you were often beaten by your brothers and
cousins (perhaps Herr Freidmann as well?), you were always being
pestered by them. Then you ran your hand down your left arm,
which, in those old days, could have been covered with blue
splotches. It didn't seem in the least as if you felt any self-pity; I,
however, could not understand—without giving myself an exact

account—how anyone could dare to raise a hand against you, since you were only a little girl back then.—Later on, you noted as an aside, while you were either looking at something or reading something (you hardly ever looked up, and the evening went by so quickly), that you had studied Hebrew as well. On the one hand, I was amazed by this, on the other (this was only my surmise, since then it has passed through the long sieve of time); I would not have wanted to see it mentioned with such exaggerated casualness, and so secretly I was quite happy later when you were unable to translate Tel Aviv.—Then it emerged that you are a Zionist, which also made me very happy.—In that same room we also talked about your profession, and Frau Brod mentioned that she had noticed a lovely batiste dress in your hotel room, as just then you were going to some wedding somewhere—I'm just guessing now, as I don't remember at all—in Budapest. Then you got up from your seat, and I saw that you were wearing Frau Brod's slippers, as you had taken off your boots to dry. The entire day, the weather had been abominable. The slippers irritated you a bit, because after we had passed through the darkened middle room, you told me that you were used to wearing slippers with heels. For me, such slippers were something new.—In the music room you sat across from me, and I began to spread out my manuscript. I received comic advice from all as to how I should send it off, but I no longer remember what you prescribed. I do, however, recall something else from the other room, causing such amazement in me that I struck my hand down on the table. There, namely, you were speaking of how you gain such pleasure from copying manuscripts, just then you were copying a manuscript for a certain gentleman in Berlin (how cursedly awful these words sound with no name or explanation appended to them!) and you asked Max to send manuscripts to you.—That evening, my most glorious deed was that I had inadvertently brought along one of the issues of *Palästina*, and for that, you can forgive me everything. We spoke of the trip to Palestine, you gave me your hand, or, to express it better, on the strength of an impulse, I coaxed it forth.—We were still listening to the piano, I was sitting diagonally behind you, you had crossed your legs, and adjusted your coiffure, which I cannot conjure up now from the front, I only know that during the piano playing it curled out a bit to one side.—Later on, the company became fairly dispersed, Frau Brod was daydreaming on the canapé, Herr Brod puttered around the bookcase, Otto struggled with the fire screen. Mention was made of Max's books, you said a few words about Arnold Beer, the critique that appeared in *Ost und West*, and then, while you were turning over the pages of one of the volumes of the Goethe series published by Propyläen, announced that you had begun reading *Nornepygge Castle*, although you could not finish it. Hearing this remark, I froze, for myself, for you, for all of us. What was the use of this superfluous affront, in no way explicable? But you saved yourself from this seemingly inescapable situation heroically as we gazed at your head, bent over the book. It turned out that this is not a matter of neither affront nor judgement, but that you were merely relating a fact at which you yourself were amazed, and therefore, you had also decided that, when the opportunity presented itself, you would once again take up the book. You could not have found a more elegant solution, and I thought that we all ought to have been a bit ashamed of ourselves.—Herr Director Brod, in order to amuse us, brought in one of the illustrated volumes of the previously mentioned Propyläen series, and announced that he would show us Goethe in his underwear. You replied with a quotation: 'He is a king, even in his underwear,' and that quotation was the one thing of which I disapproved in you that evening. I felt the pressure in my throat from my resentment gathered there, and as a matter of fact I should have asked myself why I was so sensitive in this matter. But I express myself very imprecisely.—Then, at the end, when you quickly glided out of the room and returned already in your boots, I could not get over my amazement. Frau Brod compared you to a gazelle twice, but I was not pleased by the simile.—I can see you fairly clearly even now, as you put your hat on, and stuck in the hat pin. It was a fairly large hat, white on the bottom.—We had hardly come out onto the street when I fell into that dazed state, not infrequent for me, in which I perceive only one thing clearly: my own uselessness. In Perlgasse, you asked me where I live, clearly trying to help me out of my painful muteness and because you naturally wanted to know if my walk home would take me by your hotel; whereas I, unfortunate blockhead, asked if you were curious about my address, certainly because I believed that, as soon as you got home to Berlin, you would immediately hurry to write me about the trip to Palestine and didn't want to be in the painful situation of not having my address close at hand. As I followed you, of course, I was evermore troubled by the next section of our walk, if there was even anything left in me to be troubled.—Already, upstairs in the first room, then again on the street, there was talk of a certain gentleman from your firm's Prague branch; he'd taken you up to

Hradschin that afternoon in a carriage. I felt this gentleman made it impossible on my behalf to appear the next morning at the train station with a bouquet of flowers in my hand, although for a while this intention had been hovering vaguely in my mind. That you were setting off so early, and that at such an early hour it would be impossible to get any flowers, greatly lightened my renunciation. On Obstgasse and the Graben, it was mainly Dir. Brod who was speaking, you only mentioned that your mother has the front door opened for you when you clap your hands; you remain in my debt for something of an explanation with regards to this story. Otherwise, we disgracefully wasted time comparing the Prague and Berlin transport systems. Mention was also made, if I am not mistaken, of how you took tea in the Repräsentationshaus across from the hotel. In the end, Herr Brod provided you with good instructions for the route, enumerating several stops where you could get something to eat. But you were intending to take your breakfast in the dining car. Then I also heard that you'd forgotten your umbrella in the train, and this minor detail (for me, it is a minor detail) enriched the picture I had of you with newer hues.—It concerned me greatly that you had not yet packed, and you still wanted to read in bed. The previous evening as well, you had read until four in the morning. You had taken with yourself, as reading material, Björnson's *Flags over City and Harbour* and Andersen's *Picture Book without Pictures*. I had the feeling that I too could have come up with these books, but the truth is, I never would have been capable. As we entered the hotel, in my bashfulness, I stepped into the same section of the revolving door as you, nearly trampling on your heel. Then we all stood before the elevator, in front of the waiter, the elevator into which you would disappear in a moment, the door was already open. You motioned to the waiter with a proud little speech—if I stop, I can still hear the sound of your words. You did not allow yourself to be easily convinced that no carriage was needed to reach the nearby train station. Clearly you thought you would be departing from the Franz Josef Bahnhof.—Then we said a final farewell, and I, in the clumsiest way possible, once again brought up the trip to Palestine, but already in that moment I felt I had, all evening, been mentioning this trip much too frequently, a trip which in all probability no one, part from myself, took seriously.

Felice and the Applause

We see Felice in the north-eastern quarter of Berlin as she walks along the cobblestoned streets. Her hat is black, below it is lined with white. Her face is long, her figure tall and bony. This can be seen in her clothing as well. It is careful and well maintained; the garb of a petty-bourgeois. A Fräulein, as they say. Her mouth is conspicuously strong, the lips and the area around the mouth dominates the face. Her teeth are large and white, gleaming like horses' teeth when she speaks. When she smiles, the teeth jut out, the pinkish gums are exposed. Somehow this glimmering pinkish flesh, which tends to be discreetly hidden on the faces of other people, is naked and indecent. When she speaks, Felice tries to hold her hand in front of her mouth, trying to conceal her laughter. In her handbag, next to the Pyramidon, is Franz's most recent letter. She hasn't had time to read it yet. She has to go back to her workplace before heading out to the Metropole Theatre. Walking along Leipziger Straße, she takes out the letter, tearing the envelope open, which Franz doesn't approve of—she should use a letter-opener instead, cutting along the edge carefully and circumspectly, so that afterward it will be easy to slip the folded letter back into the envelope. But no, Felice rips it open carelessly, a little impatient and irritated, wondering again what unpleasant surprise it might contain, but also with some excitement and curiosity: the letter came, after all, from her intended, who, no matter how much of an odd and peculiar figure he seemed, was still, out of all the men she had met and conversed with, flirted with and come to know over the past few years, the only one who was seriously and genuinely interested. There had been wooers before who seemed interested in her at first, but it always turned out that they wished to know more about her workplace or one of her girlfriends, mostly Greta. Felice's connections quickly ran out, the encounters fell flat: there remained time spent in the theatre with a coffee beforehand and a short stroll home afterward. In reality, Felice was bored by stage drama. The works of German classical theatre were alien to her. The Jewish theatre, which her acquaintances referred to as 'jargon theatre', wrinkling up their noses, was for her, in its remoteness, more threatening than engaging: the troubled Jewish past made her feel shame, although she didn't understand why. Franz was the only one, maniacally writing his letters, demanding a response. In the beginning, he sent his letters by registered mail, so that Felice would in no way feel she didn't have to reply to each one separately, so that if she'd received several letters in one day, she could not, with one single letter, respond to the two, three, or four letters that had arrived that day. Then Franz calmed down, but still kept an eye on everything: Felice's daily routine, her acquaintances, her work and other preoccupations. Slowly, he moved into Felice's workplace, her apartment, her room at home, his letters were lying around everywhere, the corners of his letters stuck out of Felice's disorganized handbag, from her office-desk drawers. Felice could not look anywhere without being reminded of Prague, the Worker's Accident Insurance Institute, of the impossibly tall figure who wrote her these letters, posed questions, weighed heavily on her and who, in his letters, wrote down and rewrote everything that he thought and felt so that she too would feel and think everything that Franz wrote in his letters arriving day after day. Sometimes she could hardly catch her breath, she felt she was being suffocated by his clinging, by the childish trust of this man who seemed much younger but who was already past the age of thirty, who looked to be about twenty or twenty-one years old; at the beginning, Felice thought him much too young for her. Felice had headaches in the afternoons now too. She took a tablet from the Pyramidon that she carried in her handbag. Now, as she strolled home along Immanuelkirchstraße, where she lived with her parents, she felt vexed as always when she recalled that her mother still had not given her a house key, even though she was an adult woman already, ready to start her own family, and yet she still had to clap her hands in front of the door to send the signal that she had got back home. Kafka imagines the scene, but does not hear the clapping. He never hears the clapping, in vain does he listen intently into the silent evening: he can hear his mother's wheezing, his father snoring, even the sounds of the street below. Perhaps, he suspects, Felice doesn't even clap her hands. Then how does she get into the apartment, or maybe she has a key already, and she claps her hands instead as a signal to her mother, that she has got home and now her mother can go to sleep.

Photograph Taken with a Flash

The outside of the envelope reveals nothing, a person rips it open as if it only contained a letter (and some letters arrive precisely like that, already opened, due to the construction of the envelope), but this one had a picture in it, and you yourself come sliding out, just as on a beautiful day you will step out of the railway carriage before me. This photograph taken with a flash is mine now, my dear, either temporarily or forever, as it may work out. And so that I may dispel your doubts (and not cause any newer ones), I am sending you a flash photograph of myself. It is a dreadful picture, although not intended for you: it was prepared for my power of attorney for official purposes and is at least two or three years old. In reality, my features are not so deformed, I only have such a visionary gaze by the light of a flashbulb, and I have not worn high collars for a long time.

My suit, however, is that one piece of clothing often mentioned by me (to say it is my one item of clothing is of course an exaggeration, but not by much), and even today I don it just as cheerfully as I did back then. I have caused a sensation with it

in the elegant seats of Berlin theatres, in the first row of the
Kammerspiele, and slept through entire nights, or dozed off in
train seats, wearing it. It grows old with me. Of course, the suit is
no longer as beautiful as in the photograph. I got the fancy cravat
on a trip to Paris, not even my second trip, but my first, and
suddenly I'm not even be able to tell you what year it was. By
happenstance, I'm wearing this necktie now, as I write to you. That
too grows old with me. To put it briefly, all I ask is for you is to
not be frightened by this photograph. In the past two years, there
has only been one good photograph taken of myself (the only

good photograph is one that shows a person as they would like to be seen, if there is no other way), that picture, however, is inside a frame with the other family portraits. But I will have one taken especially for you, if possible: it is very important to me that I be in your hands at least as a photograph, I mean in your true hands, as I have already been in your imaginary hands for a very long time.

The Cemetery of Language

Sometimes, when he was a little boy, Kafka went with his father to the cemetery. He did not understand anything of what was going on there. In the Jewish cemetery, there were just stones and stones everywhere. He learnt that the signs engraved into the stones were letters. However, he still didn't know how to read these letters. Even later, he got only as far as recognizing the individual letters, and he listened to them as if they were a musical scale, he read them as a foreign melody. Even later, he could never draw any lessons from them. He saw that letters are the cemetery of words. That the signs carved into the stone signify the dead. Language is a cemetery which swallows the dead into itself. There is nothing which can lead them away from here. This stone has been prepared for you, says the gravestone, here are the signs upon it.

Kafka and the Blind

Ever since Kafka had been a child, he'd felt a morbid dread of the sight of hands. Even the sight of his own hands distressed him. If he could, he tried to conceal his hands. When he was with Otto Baum, Oskar's brother, he always felt perfectly at ease, because Otto had lost his eyesight in childhood. The walks he took across the Čech Bridge and through the Kleinseite often led him past the Institute for the Blind, and every time he wondered why the building had so many windows. He never saw anyone looking out of the windows, he never saw the many heads of the inhabitants as with other public institutions. The memory of the Madhouse, which he had seen in childhood, passing by on strolls with his parents, was still very strong in Kafka's mind. The sight of the barred windows, the shaven heads of the insane, their lunatic, rounded eyes both repulsed and drew his gaze at the same time. He recalled their mouths, the dark cavities, the enormous teeth. He did not recall their maniacal speech, because as they passed, he stopped up his ears with his hands so as not to hear—not the insane, but his father, who employed this occasion to revile not only these unfortunates but Franz himself, in the form of humiliation disguised as a lecture. Then and there he understood why the house of the insane had windows facing onto the street, why there were iron bars on the windows and why there were shaved heads pressed between the grid of the window bars. His father, he realized, had arranged all this, he had requested that his tax revenue be directed to this purpose, so he could show all this to his son. But why were there windows on this building, Franz thought, every time he walked by. Why was it inconceivable that the blind would look out in the same way, and see things just as we see pictures, about which we hypothesize that they are located beyond the window, although we have no proof of that whatsoever.

That is what happens to those who scorn everything. Those who do not live by the rules are overtaken by the curse.

What curse, asked Franz, because he had already heard so much from his father about these curses. This was some kind of Jewish thing, he thought: troubled words murmured in distant and unknown synagogues. At that time—during his adolescence—Kafka was very distant from these Jewish things of which he knew very little, for the most part almost nothing, only accompanying his father to synagogue when Hermann was expected to make an appearance before the community of believers with his son. Franz would have been all too happy to deprive his father of those laudatory moments, for which, nearly humiliating himself, Hermann begged him, and in the father's gaze there was also a kind of lurking fear engendered by shame: what if they knew that his son resisted him in even such a simple matter as this, on these four occasions of the year when he went to synagogue. Franz felt his own strength draining from the father's gaze, he pitied him, this ruthless merchant, who always took what he wanted, always made a respectable profit and never ended up the loser in any deal. But now, faced with his son, he felt lost, all of his abilities vanished; Hermann sensed his luck had run out. He'd always believed in his own strength of will; by means of this willpower, he could overcome difficulties, conquer any obstacle. But the curse was something his father carried from the village where he was born, and Hermann was powerless against curses. And he suspected that this was, for his son, the obscure and mysterious curse. Or he himself was a curse for his son, it was hard to decide which. What remained certain was the uncertainty, the bad feeling, the anxious, grey obscurity that sunk into his eyes, deposited somewhere around the region of his heart, making something there get stuck.

A curse is always realized by a person upon his own self, Hermann replied sharply; he didn't like it when his son started arguing with him, as he felt it to be an attack. He didn't like this kind of sterile reasoning, which, however, his own father had loved so much. Hermann liked things that could be grasped with both hands; he'd been able to pursue his trade with such success because he'd been horrified for an entire lifetime by the example of his father's abstract conjectures. That is why he was never too happy to go to synagogue, where those Jews who thought themselves erudite sat around pondering the words of the Torah and the Talmud. Hermann had never wanted to be a Jew.

If the Lord wants to punish someone, then He takes away his reason, said his father, raising his finger. His gesture was like the rabbis', hand squeezed into a fist, index finger pointing to the sky, emphasizing his words.

You're no scholar of the Talmud, Hermann, you never even read the Talmud.

I still know what's in it, his father replied sharply. The Lord wanted to punish Nebuchadnezzar, and so He took away his reason. It's there in the Torah. For years, he climbed on his hands and knees across the closed inner courtyard of the palace. He grazed on grass, he pooped squatting on the ground, he drank his own pee, the fool . . .

Where did you get that from, the mother asked, with her most endearing and submissive smile: she wanted to disarm her husband, to reconcile him with his son by diverting the conversation; the lurking tension between father and son threatened to explode. It was the mother who mediated between father and son. The mother who bore the burden of the father's dissatisfaction, because this boy brought shame upon him. Just as it was the mother who dissolved the son's rage, transforming it into an understanding of the father: that rage that made the boy the father's son. The son felt he was a debtor to his father. This debt would last for his entire life and could never be paid off; not because of the life he had been given, although it was truly his mother who had done that—she had carried him—instead, it was a question posed by the father which, the son realized evermore as the years passed by, he was obligated to answer. He would need to gather all his strength to reply, a strength he felt he didn't have, and perhaps never would.

That isn't in the Talmud. Although maybe that's what they taught you in the cheder, said the mother, back in the village, she added, but playfully, because any mention of the distance between the world of Hermann and that of Julie was an eternal point of contention between them. In Kafka's imagination, their two childhoods existed like two separate islands: Hermann's, rough and ignorant, and Julie's, refined, conversant in the ways of the capital city; ever since their marriage, these two islands were floating away from each other, growing evermore distant. Franz did not see himself on either of these islands.

The shaven heads and the lunatic gazes. The temptation—he only had to be like them, and he could be finally left alone with his papers, busy himself with his writing instruments—filled Franz with fear. If he could simulate insanity, he wouldn't have to go to the office any more or complete tasks of no interest, about which he suspected evermore—indeed, he was coming to believe—that it was all the result of a conspiracy orchestrated by his father. Although his office job did exempt him from having to work in his father's shop, since he was a civil servant. His father would have also liked to see him spend more time in the factory, but Franz was interested in the factory least of all. The factory, where he had set foot once unsuspectingly, because the father had, with shrewd extortion, persuaded him to visit his brother-in-law, employing his usual tricks as he did whenever he sensed he might suffer a rout vis-a-vis his loved ones; the father made himself weak, like one of those false beggars hypocritically pleading for the small change of sympathy: once they get it, however, they gaze maliciously at the departing giver, despising that arrogance, clothed in pity, that just now swindled them. The father, a cunning and calculating merchant, took Franz in with one his sneaky tricks, when Franz provisionally agreed to his request—more of an extortion—to visit the factory, presumably to assist his brother-in-law and sister, although to call the place a factory was to varnish the truth, as it reminded Franz much more of a correctional facility; he'd gained a notion of such facilities during the course of his law studies, leading him to conclude that the primary goal behind the disciplining and maiming of the body was the torture of the soul. Factories, as institutions of detainment, were much cheaper to run than penitentiaries, as well as producing greater profit, Franz realized, and finally these insights also lay behind his decision to work at an institution that protected the legal rights of these prisoners and workers, providing them with material help, at least according to popular belief and to all appearances.

In the factory—purchased by his father, run by his brother-in-law, and where asbestos was produced—Franz once again confronted the source of his own comfortable existence, something he would have preferred to forget but did not have the strength to renounce, along with all the advantages of his own inherently privileged situation, felt as natural by him ever since childhood. The factory was an island of hopelessness; as Franz walked in, the full weight of his father's disgraceful arrogance came crashing down on him again, that disgraceful arrogance that kept the people working here under degrading circumstances, fobbing them off with ridiculous wages. And in reality, Franz stealthily watched his father from an adjoining room as he hoodwinked the workers, blinding them with fraudulent words, wringing his hands, lamenting how the factory was running at a loss: he only kept it open out of compassion and pity for them and their families who only took his earnings from the shop, money that he gained by the sweat of his brow. In the shop, where, as he always said, he worked for his family from dawn to dusk, for that ungrateful, bloodsucking gang.

Hermann, who, like all people bursting with health, turned away in dread from every illness, unable to withstand the sight of a maimed human body; he fainted easily, like women. That is why he never could have continued his father's trade; he was never happy to walk into the butchery, and even when he did it was only with head bowed, so as not to see the bloody animal parts hanging down from the hooks.

The Enigma of the Sphinx

When the Swollen-Footed reached the crossroads, something happened which he almost didn't notice, only realizing its significance much later on. A stranger coming towards him in this barren and desolate region began commenting on his feet, letting drop a remark about the Swollen-Footed's strange, flattened nose; this remark remained in his memory only because as the Swollen-Footed, his hatred quickly rising, knocked down the distinguished man with such force that his short sword lacerated his skull, he saw, as he lay on the ground, in the middle of the bleeding face, a nose almost perfectly identical to his own—the nose for which the Swollen-Footed had been mocked since childhood. No one else had a nose like that. It was this nose, perhaps, that had elicited such sudden and inexplicable rage, such a murderous impulse from the Swollen-Footed as he heard the stranger's arrogant comments, at first mocking, then disparaging, and finally—the Swollen-Footed did not respond, but remained obstinately silent—calumnious. Due to his childhood injuries, the Swollen-Footed always carried a cane, but used it only when tired. Now, exhausted from his long wanderings, he was limping, and when the man and his servant saw him, the man, turning to his servant, remarked: Here comes a three-legged animal, because people are two-legged, or in childhood, they are four-legged. The Swollen-Footed was silent; he stopped, waiting for them to pass, but the man, pleased with his own foolish ingenuity, stopped to ask the Swollen-Footed: What kind of an animal are you, where did you come from and where you going?

Later on, the Swollen-Footed realized: his own silence was why he had to kill the arrogant man and the servant, goading his master to further calumny: he was so thirsty and exhausted that he had no desire to speak, and so did not converse with the insolent, flat-nosed man. His silence could have been taken for arrogance or disrespect, although it was neither. His fear arose from that curse, the childhood prophecy that he would murder his father in a sudden rage. The Swollen-Footed was prone to sudden rages, he knew this about himself, and when he encountered the man and his servant, there was still, in his convulsively clenched mouth, the cry he'd stifled when he nearly slayed his father at home, before he ran away to the great wide world. This cry of horror at the gods' curse made the Swollen-Footed mute, and so he could not converse with the self-confident and conceited man, his affluence evident from his garments, and the servant whom the Swollen-Footed also had to kill, as he had seen everything. He looked at the two bloody corpses, the servant's mangled face, with relief, calm now: the Swollen-Footed had thrashed him with all his might, smashing his skull to pieces with abandon because the prophecy was fulfilled—he had become a murderer, killed two people, and so he no longer had to fear the curse: it was not his father he had struck dead, but merely a stranger encountered on the road to Thebes. Afterward, he never spoke to anyone about this. Not even his lover, whom he took in her widowhood, filling the King's place in the palace and in her bed. The silence filled the house: from this silence two courageous boys were born, two splendid girls—the screech of the conjugal bed and the fecundity of the city. This quietness was broken afterward only once, by silence.

Tiny Flowers on a Calico Dress

Kafka sees his father's hand squeezing the maidservant's breast, he kneads it under the dark-blue calico fabric with its pattern of small flowers. The father always had the dresses made for the servant girls from the same flower-patterned calico fabric. The girls came and went. Some stayed for years; others gave notice after one or two months. Julie never intervened. The father brought back the fabric from the shop, the end of the bolt that couldn't be sold, slightly defective material, for the girls. There were always new girls coming, the dresses had to be adjusted, new ones sewed, there were skinnier girls and stouter girls, small-breasted or large-breasted, but the fabric remained the same. Julie also liked this constancy. Hermann, for his part, insisted on it. Because of this, Franz found flowers to be repugnant, especially small ones. He saw his father's enormous hands at the Sunday dinner table clutching the knife and the fork, menacingly brandishing them to the heavens when he was famished. He grasped them in his fists, the fork in his left hand and the knife in his right, impatient and alert. His hands gripped the family silver to which, following

Czech custom, Julie's parents had added a few pieces for the young couple. Just as they had done with the porcelain service. It was part of their common assets, including taxes and duties paid to the state.

When is the girl coming already, he would yell to Julie on the other side of the table, as if it was up to this humble woman, her head bent, to solve the situation at once. Hermann's hunger was always intolerable; someone had to satisfy it immediately. When he yelled like this, Julie coughed discreetly and cleared her throat, which did not drown out her husband's yelling; she tapped the side of her glass with her knife. Later, she placed a handbell on the table to her left; she discreetly rang it. At one point, Hermann got a table bell from somewhere, the kind placed on the counter in restaurants where many waiters dash around, jumping at the customers' commands: kindly light my cigar, son, bring me the *Prager Tagblatt*, run over to the post office to fetch my telegram. The waiters jot down the orders on a slip of paper, leaving it by a small counter window, then quickly tap the bell before running off again. That sound is enough for a hand to reach out through the small window; it snaps up the slip of paper, sliding the window closed again. Franz saw these hands flying back and forth in his mind's eye.

The most terrifying hands were the ones right in front of Franz. He saw his father's hand as it pinched the cook's bottom, stealthily, so Julie wouldn't notice. The cook had an enormous backside. Franz only saw his father's hand: he imagined the enormous backside traversed by shivering undulations as it stepped, the two buttocks sliding up and down, down and up.

Hermann could not stop pinching her backside. With time, the cook began to expect it, turning to grant the master of the house a chance to exercise what he considered to be one of his innate prerogatives, just like the marrow bone; at the same time, though, it had to be done so that Julie, sitting at the other end of the table, wouldn't notice. Or at least in such a way that allowed Julie to pretend she hadn't noticed. Franz, sitting to the right of Hermann, saw everything precisely. At these times, his father caught Franz's gaze, and he winked at him complicitly. This made Franz even more troubled; he lowered his eyes. He felt revulsion rising in his throat, like a bite of something badly chewed making him want to throw up. The father turned away from his son, disappointed, scowling, and, to console himself, rested his gaze upon the backside, now moving away, until it was swallowed up by the hallway door leading to the servant's room, closing shut.

Kafka and Palestine

My dear and honoured Fraulein, How differently does the phrase 'Next year in Jerusalem!' sound when it is not the youngest son who utters it, not at the Seder table, not in the voice of old Jewish piety, and not with that veiled pain with which it is uttered by Jews, but as I pronounced it to you at Max's when I reached my hand across the table. Perhaps you recall that table upon which there was nothing to remind you that there might be something about it, or those sitting around it, in common with that city that the well-to-do merchants of Prague think about while their minds are on the shop: rental expenses, expected procurement prices, bulk-purchasing discounts, profits on currency exchange when buying imported goods and monies saved from wages. Next year in Jerusalem, they say, just like my father on the evening of the Seder, and the alliance between him and my mother must once again be reinforced, at least with these words. For him, this means they are allied: that he, Hermann, the creator of our world, and Julie, my mother, the embodiment of this creating force, will continue to maintain that alliance formed when the match-maker—on the basis of a not-too-large, but also not-insignificant offer—judged that a little deal could be made by bringing these two people together; and so Hermann and Julie stepped into this eternal alliance, in the closely intertwining hope of family and business. This eternal alliance is something I myself cannot imagine, particularly if it involves children.

My dear son,

I hope that my letter finds you in good health, which I, with your mother, wish for you very much in Berlin, because the weather there, although not worse than here, is more unpredictable, and it is always easier to put up with something you're used to as opposed to something you don't exactly know. If we may make one request of you: please be careful in your choice of clothing, and never believe, if you look out the window in the morning and see the sun shining, that it will be shining all day. In Berlin, the weather is much more uncertain and changeable than in our good old Prague, which is what your frail organism has been used to, for nearly forty years now. Your mother and I both know how hard it is to give you advice, because you always take it as something directed against you. You must know that for us Jews, it is difficult, almost impossible to believe that everything really is the way the goyim think it is. For us, words mean something completely different, take, for example, someone named Green: how could he ever believe that the meadow is green, the trees and the grass are also green, and that finally green is in reality just a word, if anything at all can be green?

When it comes to most things, we Jews, as you wrote in your letter, believe that someone wrote them down. This is true, even when we don't read enough—something with which you rebuke me, and your dear mother as well, who is the least deserving of such admonitions from you. I have been reading for my entire life, everything I've ever had to deal with—trade, bargaining, buying and selling—all of this was nothing but reading. But this is your hobbyhorse, so there's no point in trying to explain.

But you wouldn't about know this, my dear son, because you're not even Jewish, you were never chased by the other boys in the school courtyard as they yelled in your ear 'Stand still, Jewish dog!' to cut off your ear locks. When did you ever even once have to stand up for the ones they call Jews, as if you ever had anything to do with the affairs of others for whom you are punished because you happen to be right there, and you are identified with those about whom no one can imagine that they don't even exist? Because people never want to know the truth, they only believe what they themselves have created. The only difference is that the goyim create something that can be grasped whereas the Jews kept believing in something distant and intangible. Your mother, who sets the table for you every day, knows this, as do I; at the Sabbath table, though, your place is left empty, and a chalice is set out every Sabbath for Elijah, as if every Sabbath were itself the Seder, the meal held in memory of the Exodus, and you sit there only as a body, your soul having wandered off a long time ago. Because of that, the Seder so sorrowful is in our house.

And yet, as you know, I do not think very much of what the Jews do, I don't care much for forms: what's important for me are textiles, the material, the form as it is sewn. I'm only interested in materials, in patterns as they emerge on the fabric. Of course, you could say I'm superficial, you and your friends, that we Jews only are preoccupied with the surface and not with the depth, as you might expect us to be. In reality, what is depth, can you tell me? And what can you expect from a textile merchant who has spent his entire life handling the surface of fabrics? If I were to go blind—which, given my worsening eyesight, is evermore likely with the passing of years—I would be still able to identify every fabric on the basis of touch. Sometimes I can sense colours: red is warmer than blue, brown is softer than yellow—this is certainly just some kind of superstition, you would certainly say, a superstition. Well, and the vegetarianism you're so proud of, you take a stand against me with that too, isn't that also a superstition? Well, and what about everything that Rudolf Steiner talks about, traipsing all over Europe for the snobs who can afford it? And isn't that literature you pursue with those friends of yours also a superstition? Once again, I've only managed to get myself irritated, and I can't argue with you.

Lichtgasse

When Kafka was a child, his father didn't live in the same street in which he worked. The father left in the morning, the son watching from the window. If the weather was good, he was allowed to go down to the street and wave after him. The father walked along, his high shoulders concealing the sun. The child, little Franz, looked up to him, he saw his father as a giant, and in reality, he was a giant compared to tiny Franz. Hermann Kafka ambled along; his walking stick, overlaid with copper, tapped along the cobblestones. It was red copper, because that was more distinguished. Namely, it was rarer. Whatever was rare was more distinguished, Hermann Kafka taught his children. A sparrow is common, it chirps everywhere, said Hermann Kafka, pointing at the bushes which stood at the end of the garden. They were elder-berry, unassuming elderberry bushes, not even real bushes, because their branches, when they first grew out, were soft and milk-like, becoming firmer only with time. The dried-out branches remained spongy on the inside for a long time, like sunflower stalks, although it was a perennial. Kafka used to hide under them, he liked to climb in-between the branches and imagine he was a bird. The father did not want his son's attention to go wandering among the swallows, the elderberry bushes, the world of fragrances and imagination, and so he touched his son's head, caressing it as men do children's heads, with restraint and a little coldly, just as when they barter in the market or the shop, offering textiles to each other or to a customer; Hermann Kafka would caress the surface of the fabric with a kind of restrained refinement, as if he didn't need it, as if he weren't even really touching it, because he wanted to bargain down the price, to depreciate the fabric, list its defects, everything he could and didn't even have to say. That was how Kafka now caressed his son's head, so that with this movement, he would redirect his son's thoughts and attention back into the present, because he knew what a great danger the past was for Jews, he had to protect his son from the past: he caressed his son's head so that he would take full notice of his father, the father to whom otherwise respectful attention must be paid at all times if he is speaking or about to do so. The father also knew that even more threatening than the past, for the Jews, was the future lying in wait for them. The responsibility of a father was to protect his children from the future that might steal his child from him, most probably his son, always of utmost importance to a Jewish father, for his very life is his son; and death is his own father. That is why Hermann Kafka knew that for his son, the father—in other words, himself—meant death. And that is why the father did not wish for a son, but instead for the son of his son, a grandson. That is why Abraham sacrificed Isaac, who bleated like a goat so that Jacob could be born: through him, Isaac would receive the blessing.

Hermann loved his son, but he also desired this unknown grand-son. Hermann behaved with his son as most fathers do: he did not understand him, he only loved him, and because he loved him, he could not do anything else than wish to protect him from everything he himself feared. He accepted, as the decree of the Almighty, that Franz was his son, because although he was not a religious Jew, the faith of others caused no doubts within him. His doubts were connected to the faith of the Jews in the very least, the Christians [ ]

Most streets have two ends. Even blind alleys, which can only be entered or exited from one direction. The lines, whether they be straight or curved, [ ]

Why are you hiding from me, asked Hermann. Why do you go climbing through those dark alleyways when there are no longer any ghettos in Prague? Why do you long for the ghetto again when it took our ancestors centuries to get out of there?

I do not long for the ghetto. The ghetto is within us, we lived within it for so long that it moved into us, said Franz.

His son's words irritated Hermann, his bent head as he listened, the resignation with which he replied. If only he weren't so weak. He wasn't manly enough. And what can remain to a man if not his dignity? Money is like sunshine—sometimes it's there, sometimes it isn't. You can never trust it. Only the goyim think money is an end in and of itself. Hermann had learnt that money is an instrument. A man does not believe in money, he can only believe in dignity, recognized by the community. If someone is wealthy, his wealth is a means of gaining prestige. But that too must be guarded. And this was exactly what was lacking in Franz: he never exerted himself for the dignity or authority that comes with recognition. He wasn't even interested in money. Because he'd always had everything, Hermann, who had started out as a barefoot child, fumed to himself: he'd had to fight his siblings for a crust of bread. Franz's mother was weak, a shrinking violet from the city. His mother, he grumbled to himself. Franz had inherited his mother's nature; this is my curse.

But still, my son. There's no reason for you to go hiding in these dark alleyways. To make friends with strange and troubled young people who are only so enthusiastic and rage-filled, because they're jealous. They're jealous of those who have something. If someone has money, they're jealous of the money. If someone has knowledge, they're jealous of the knowledge. If someone has a beautiful wife, they're jealous of the wife. If someone is talented, then they're jealous of the talent. Don't believe them. They lie, they say they're revolutionaries, but they aren't. They say they're artists, but they are the soldiers of fortune in this new world—in the old days they would have been thronging the royal court, becoming either executioners or victims.

My father always lived in Lichtgasse, said Franz.

A Cloudy Day

We see Kafka, Franz Kafka, as he walks along the Großer Ring. His shadow is drawn upon the grid of the cobblestones. It could be afternoon, an autumnal afternoon. Late autumn. The lights are sharp, as if there were a breeze. The Großer Ring is like a photograph traversed by Herr Doctor, as he is addressed in the office. His lanky frame totters in the wind. It isn't his height that makes him look so lanky, but his body's stupefying gauntness. He is so thin that anyone observing him could only imagine bones beneath his overcoat—not the connective tissues holding the skeleton together, and especially not superfluous organs such as the stomach, the dreadful labyrinth of the intestines, the liver, the heart—not even the lungs, expanding, claiming evermore space. Only the bones can withstand this gauntness, ghastly and improbable. The sterile white bones. The figure in the photograph evokes a weather-beaten mast, its sail hanging down. The black canvas sail droops below the knees. For the simile to fit perfectly, Kafka only has to raise his arms and spread them apart. Even without doing so, the figure's lowered right shoulder and the slightly pulled-up left shoulder together look like a mast with its horizontally crossing lines. Kafka buttons his coat up carefully so that his chest, more precisely the lungs positioned in orderly fashion inside his chest, will be protected.

'Franz, button up your coat,' Hermann had called after him that morning, his thoughts already preoccupied with business. He is dissatisfied with the assistants, already dissatisfied although he is still at home. When he steps into the shop, the small bell tinkling above the door, the tittering will stop, but no one will dare look at him. They will receive his curses in silence. These curses already lie behind Hermann's words: 'Franz, button up your coat,' burning like embers. Franz now senses that his coat is buttoned up too tightly. His throat feels as if it is being squeezed. It's as if the wind isn't as sharp as it was this morning when he walked to the office, he thinks.

'Good morning, Herr Doctor,' the porter greets him, clicking his heels together, his uniform tightly buttoned, the fabric stretched tightly across his potbelly. The Insurance Company porter is Czech but, out of sheer courteousness, he greets Kafka in German. Franz replies in Czech, out of obliging attentiveness. The postal clerk also chases away the Insurance Company's clients in Czech. For the most part, the workers are Czech. The stubborn and hopeless cases. Franz thinks that the porter only knows enough German to greet him, or perhaps he understands everything? He wonders about this while he lingers in front of the porter, pondering, not knowing if he should keep moving or remain standing there. He must empathize with every employee of the firm. As the motto goes these days: 'Solidarity to the personnel, to whom we are beholden.' How much are we beholden to them, and since when, Kafka thinks to himself. Maybe he should say something else to this person clicking his heels together in a military fashion, standing respectfully at attention before him. His posture isn't as tight as a soldier's: there's a certain homely slovenliness in his stance, a Czech ingratiating familiarity reminiscent of the old Austrian monarchy, a peaceful civilian sloppiness. This man certainly used to be a soldier, perhaps the fleeting thought occurs to Franz. He was one of that kind. Kafka knows well that such jobs, confidential positions, as they are called, comfortable, gentlemanly, necessitating contact with the common folk on a daily basis, could only be had in exchange for something. You have to earn it. Do something else beyond being a porter.

He spent the day as he did every day in the office, which was a form of death for him. And it was the same for everyone else, Kafka used to say to his friends—only that the great majority of people don't realize they have sunk to depths of servitude and turpitude from where nothing more can be seen. Among those who awaken for a few moments from the stupefaction that is called life these days, in that seemingly dead state to which modern nations exile their citizens, only very few are aware of this.

When it was two o'clock in the afternoon, Franz stood up: the day was done. He compared the time on his wristwatch to the settings of the hands of the grandfather clock in the office. He breathed a sigh of relief. He went to his new room, rented on a monthly basis; it had been arranged by Ottla, a place for him to continue his real work, the work for which he was born in this world. He went to his newest studio, located in the Goldenes Gäßchen. He only returned home late at night. When he got there, he lay down on the narrow divan, falling into a light and refreshing sleep. At last, in that space of solitude and silence, sleep came to him as a reward for the sufferings of the day. When he awoke, it was as if he were surfacing from the ocean's depths, he gasped for breath, eyes wide open, then, sitting down at the table by the light filtering in through the tiny window, he began to write. He wrote slowly, the muscles in his hand were tired; he stared into the distance for a long time, ruminating on some never-glimpsed distance. Then he continued, scratching out the lines one beneath the other. The writing slowly dissolved the tension within him; his eyebrows, knotted from sleep, smoothed out, the furrow carving a long arc into his forehead began to clear. Now it was not as deep or harsh. He began to breathe more easily, the rattling sound emerging from his lungs, intensifying in his mouth cavity, disappeared.

The gentle evening air tempted Kafka to take a longer stroll than usual. Although he liked to walk across Charles Bridge, now he went farther, traversing the Čech Bridge to the Old Town: from afar, he could see the apartment houses intended to make the traces of the ghetto disappear. He glimpsed the building 'Zum Schiff', where their old apartment had been located, from a distance. Every time he walked by it, he always looked up to the window of his old room, making him think of the years he'd spent there, most of all of Felice: Felice, whom he'd tried to chain to himself by means of writing, as Felice herself had once reproached him; Felice to whom he wished, through writing, to chain himself so that that guilty conscience embittering his life with those ballast weights known as Felice would bind him to life. On Niklasstraße, the recently constructed boulevard built in the New Style, which the residents of Prague affectionately called Pariser Straße, its arrow-straight route and luxurious secessionist apartment blocks reminded everyone of Paris, everyone who wished they could leave Prague, more precisely it reminded them of the lovely former scenes of their lives. The boulevard led directly to the square in the heart of the Old Town, which the German residents, as well as the Jews who had been moved out of the ghetto, called the Großer Ring, while the Czechs referred to it as Old Town Square. For Kafka, this square was where his parents had relocated to from the apartment house 'Zum Schiff'. His window didn't look out onto the square but onto the adjacent Russian Church, the Niklaskirche, in Russian possession until the end of the war.

Years earlier, one day, he had stood for a long time underneath the window of 'Zum Schiff' and felt that he had no other possibility than to allow the earth pull him to itself—the earth which the Slavs called 'little mother'—it would enfold him to itself; finally, like a great embrace, it would take him into itself, enveloping him, as it did everyone who had ever been born. He remained in this final and redemptive possibility, as he felt there was no other way forward: marriage had not worked out, the idea of having a child was inconceivable to him, he could not make someone who wasn't even born yet unhappy when they still could escape from the suffering he would cause, he'd already made enough trouble for the living through dishonour. In the silence of the evening, he heard the clattering of his heart, he sensed the blood pumped into his veins by this heart which had not yet stopped serving his body, he heard the distant clock towers as they marked the quarter hour, than a half-hour, then three quarters of an hour and then finally the hour. Then everything began again from the beginning. He listened to the distant noises, to the sound of his heart prized open from his body. He looked at the sky and the river, the beckoning pavement down below beneath his feet. On that evening he was completely close to something, the irresolvable contradictions.

The Silence of Nebuchadnezzar

Why am I so fascinated with the story of Nebuchadnezzar, in which there is nothing grand or uplifting, and not even the escape from expected despair fills me with joy? Why do I feel that there is a kind of message for me in this story? And why do I feel it to be so much my own, when I can't even listen to it properly? I never believed that the years Nebuchadnezzar spent in utter muteness were lost. Without that curse, his empire never would have become that colossal error, captivating even in its ruins, amid that series of preconceptions known as history. Namely, history meant little to Franz: it was something he'd heard a lot of in school, and, since then, every time someone wanted to make him believe in some sacred misunderstanding. Wars are incited in the name of history. If you can believe that one. It is possible, but those raised in this way never become heroes. It was enough for Kafka to ponder this for him to feel his entire life was merely a sequence of lost years.

But were those years truly lost, those years spent in the palace's enclosed inner courtyard where no one could see him, in unconscious inactivity, panic having built its nest in his lunatic eyes? His wife had not dared approach him for a long time: when he saw her, the king began to whimper, trying to bore his head into the corner where the walls met. If he heard his beloved wife's approaching steps, he began to whine, beating his head against the expensive bricks coated with blinding white enamel. The wall pediments were edged with fire-red enamel. In the sunlight [ ], which he'd brought here from distant mountains. He had the snow-white palace constructed because of the whiteness of his wife's body. He had all this built because he could not accept that all bodies—including that single body, the most precious to him—would, one day, take on an opalescent hue, and every gaze would collapse, every naval lose its fragrant moistures, become a reeking crater. In the same way, he fled from the ruins of his kingly power. He went down on all fours so that he could renounce everything dearest to him. He did not wish to suffer defeat, namely, he had never suffered defeat.

He removed from himself every requisite of power. The expensive jewels, the clothes flung away marked his path. The king was naked, crouching on all fours, hidden from the gaze of all in the centre of the enclosed inner courtyard when, after a long search, his servants found him: he made a howling sound as they tried to approach, frightening the servants who'd previously trembled in his presence; it took them a while to realize that the once-dreaded king now feared them so much that he urinated on the ground in his torture. When the servants realized their master had been struck with a divine curse, they laughed scornfully, frightening him, teasing him onto greater trembling and panic as they laughed. When his wife saw and realized, after a short while, what was happening to her husband, she ordered everyone out of the courtyard; she had it locked with the stern command that, from this day on, no one apart from her could enter. Whining and whimpering, the king assailed her. His wife, however, was sorry for this man who had loved her so much; from that day on, she took charge of the kingdom's affairs, while the hope that she and the king might yet again sleep in one bed—as was the fitting obligation of a married couple—diminished as the days went by.

The wretched years passed. The king's hair was matted, hanging down in bunches, with more grey hairs from one day to the next. Finally, only white strands remained. His beard, almost completely grey as well, reached down to his waist. Sometimes he sat for days in a trance, not moving. There was, in the palace, a hunchbacked, simple-minded servant, tolerated as the son of one of the king's concubines. The boy was sent to take care of the horses, he fed the cows and cleared out the muck, all the undignified and repulsive tasks were given to him because he was stupid and couldn't speak. He never complained. At the request of the king's wife, the chief minister placed the boy with the king to carry out his muck and wash the enamelled tile floor of the elaborately decorated inner courtyard. The simple-minded boy had no objections. He conducted himself here just as he did in the stables. He did not recognize the king. He did not speak to him, only at times enunciating certain sounds, such as the ones he used with horses to calm them down. Sometimes the king was more restless, at the time of the new moon, or at the beginning of the rainy season. When the boy saw that the king was eating grass, he stood next to him, lowered himself on his hands and knees and began to chew the blades of grass, his head tilted to the side like a dog's or cat's. At first the king grumbled at him threateningly, then got used to him. The simple-minded boy was the only one he tolerated. When the king saw him, he did not begin to beat his head in panic against the stones. One didn't know what it was about this woeful boy that was comforting for him, but then one forgets everything. The king's wife, though, did not forget her husband: at the time of the new-year celebrations, held on the days of the lunar new year, she glided along the corridors, closed and empty for years now, and, through a single crevice known to her, pushing aside a plank in a boarded-up door, she tumbled into the courtyard now swimming in light, the trees and the flowers growing wild everywhere, overwhelming fragrances mixed in with the scent of excrement and urine. She saw no change. The king sat on the ground, his clothes long since in tatters, his precious mantle no longer reminiscent of the old light. He had torn off the jewels, tossed them away because they were inedible. He'd used his golden buckle to scratch something out of the ground, then, when he was done, thrown it away. Or buried it and forgot where. Sometimes he sniffed the earth, randomly began to scratch at it with his two hands. The king was wretched, stinking and repugnant, no one would have suspected the world's most powerful king subsisted in this human wreckage. Everyone knew he was the king; only he did not know. The body of the king, however, was sacred: no one was allowed to touch him. He withdrew from the sun into the shadows, and if it rained, slept under the sky, rolling around naked in the puddles. Years passed, and no one believed that the king could be healed. Only the simple-minded boy was faithful to him, and he spoke to no one. After a while he never left the king at all, sitting in the courtyard at a respectful distance from his master, imitating him in everything. As the years went by, he resembled the king more and more. His hair hung down in knots, his beard, already sprinkled with grey, reached down to his waist. If he sensed the impulse, he too squatted and began to shit, accompanied by loud moans, to relieve himself. When he was done, he moved a bit to the side to rest after the great exertion. The smell didn't bother him. The king slowly became used to this lone servant who asked for and communicated nothing; from one year to the next, he felt ever-greater trust in him. In these solitary, barren times, he never became fully alienated from people, for in his solitary existence he was not fully alone. And so the years passed. The lunar new year came, and the shining face of the luminous Moon god once again turned towards the forbidden courtyard of the royal palace, closed to all: the Moon glanced down at the two crouching figures in the inner courtyard.

When the king slept, the servant cleaned out the courtyard, took out the excrement, scattered sand where they had urinated and defecated, then rinsed the spot with water. He watered the plants, poured clean water into the basin. He tossed pieces of fresh fruit onto the grass, hung roasted legs of mutton from the branches of the fragrant shrubs blooming all year round. Then he went to lie down in his nest prepared from blades of grass, similar to his master's, in which he, just as the king, had hidden three egg-shaped white stones, upon which he sat every day for a long time, turning them over regularly just as birds do. No stone hatched in the nest of the king or the servant. The king began to lose his patience, he was dissatisfied. The only thing that calmed him was for him to observe sneakily, whenever he could, his servant's eggs: they also showed no signs of nestlings about to hatch. The stone birds simply did not wish to give any signals with their new-born's tiny, egg-breaking teeth.

The great king, lord of the underworld, when he had finished brooding, got up on all fours, dragged himself over to one side—his joints had grown stiff—and raising his right knee, began to urinate by a nearby bush. When he was done, his wandering gaze noticed the hanging knuckles of ham. He realized he was hungry. He clambered over on all fours and yanked down the roasted ham with his mouth, mangling it on the ground. When the servant approached, he grumbled at him. The servant, in his sudden fear, jumped up and ran away on two legs. The insane king became very confused. Not long after, he stood up on his two legs as well. He touched his body with his hands like someone looking for something. He spoke to his remorseful servant in his old voice, telling him to bring his clothes. Stand up, make a fool of yourself no more. Then he added that he—namely, the king—knew very well he was only playacting. And while it was not truly worthy of him, experience shows, although in a contradictory fashion, that the only one not to lose his mind is he who uses it correctly.

Memory of a Nearness

Whoever—from the Großer Ring, the heart of the Old Town—wishes to escape the ghosts of the city or the demons of his own heart should turn his face to the north. If, in the middle of the square, he glances up at the northern sky, he will see the luminous dawn star, the star of Lucifer. This light will guide his path no matter how confused he might be, no matter what sorrow weighs upon his heart. Perhaps his body is burning up, perhaps fear causes sweat to pour down his brow: but if he turns his face to the north, a refreshing breeze from the direction of Niklas Bridge will strike his face. The veil of vapour caresses him like the veil of a mother leaning over the bed of a feverish child: she has just come home from the cabaret to her less burdened husband. This veil still carries within itself the cool breath of the cold street and the chilly evening. And how endearing to perceive the heavy, overpowering smell of cigar smoke within it, the cigar smoke that men, their faces numb with whiskey, blow into the mother's hair as they bend above her neck, whispering into her ear something meant only for her. The mother turns her graceful, snail-shaped ear towards them;

the touch of the moustache, tickling, makes it shudder, the warm breath from the whispering mouth striking her discreetly curving ear canal, lost in the indentations of skin.

Above the Großer Ring, the weight of one of Eastern Europe's oldest nights sinks down upon the solitary evening wanderer. Perhaps the Jews, who are at home everywhere, walked on this square in the most ancient of times in Eastern Europe, because everywhere above them is the same empty gaping sky. The weight of this gaping depth—threatening to devour the world—was perhaps here the greatest, a few metres from the old ghetto, here in the distant north, where the Jews dragged their fear and dread all the way from Jerusalem. And if someone couldn't bear it any more, if the devil had taken up residence in his heart, he could escape by turning northward and running, between the tall apartment blocks, along the arrow-straight Niklasstraße, breathing a sigh of relief as he was released from the tons of weight pressing down; on the Niklas Bridge, which the Czechs called Čech Bridge, he would finally emerge above the Moldau's dignified inundations. On the other side of the river is the inviting hillside, the gardens named after Crown Prince Rudolf, offering refuge: there, he can hide from his pursuers behind the garden benches, the cherubs, and the shrubs—but he hasn't got there yet. The residents of Prague call Niklasstraße the 'suicides' ramp'. The bridge's low railing stands alluringly in the way of the unlucky, the lonely, the lost. The ones who have more feeling than the others. The ones chased by demons.

Kafka stood in front of the window and looked at the deserted Niklasstraße coming into view from behind the building. He saw those demons wandering around aimlessly on a dead evening in Prague's Old Town Square. He also would see them in the byways of the city, when, on one of his afternoon or twilight strolls, he gazed into this or that alley. He was used to their presence. And they recognized his lanky form. Now, though, the evening plunged down upon him with such force that it caused his shoulders to sag. For years now, he'd had to gather all his strength to hold himself up straight, to lift his head far enough above the evening waters to get some air. That's why he sat at his writing desk until dawn, to raise his head up a bit, to get some air. He'd been suffocating for years. He knew a deluge of filth was approaching, the smell of corpses spreading everywhere in Eastern Europe. He couldn't breathe, his lungs wheezed. His body moved, in this exertion, like plants struggling to grow in shadow. Gaunt, they try to extend themselves upward to reach some light. This strain makes them frail and defenceless: even a weak storm leaves them plastered on the ground. That's how it was for Kafka with air, he struggled for it, dragging himself all over the city, up to Hradschin, across the Moldau and back. Like an animal enclosed in its cage in the Tiergarten, he restlessly walked the streets of night-time Prague, circling around.

On the fourth floor of 'Zum Schiff', where he sleeps with the window open all year round, he now stands by the window and, with a worried gaze, looks towards Josefplatz as glinting moonlight draws lines on the cobblestones of deserted Niklasstraße; his gaze seems to be directed at the tollbooth of Niklas Bridge. In reality, though, he's looking at the water, at the depth of four stories, opening before him like a chasm, although at other times he only sees the distance. Now he sees a precipice into which he can enclose himself forever. His face is dark, his eyes ringed by deep shadows. The light falls onto him, the star of Lucifer, the brightest star in the sky, it falls upon him, as does the phosphorescent spray of the moon. And this vapour drizzles down onto the waves of the Moldau as well. The ark lamps of the Niklas Bridge, like a string of pearls, sway across to the Kleinseite, across the river of equilibrium, above which he had once walked with Felice: she put her arm in his as if they were a married couple going for a walk on a Sunday afternoon, like two people after years of a long and weary marriage, the disillusioned and broken slaves of the exigencies of bourgeois hypocrisy. If he thinks more upon it, he'd never been happier in his entire life. And he would never again be as happy.

Kafka and the Colours

Jewish family names are so unusual, Kafka thought as a child, when it occurred to him that among the family's acquaintances, not only were people named Little and Big, Fat and Gaunt, Rich and Poor, but thinking it over there were amusing colour surnames too. There were the basic colours, such as Grün, Rot, Blau, Gelb, Schwarz, and Weiß: names from which you can immediately tell that its bearer can only be Jewish. You can bet that ten to one, a hundred to one—if not even greater probability—that a family named Blau is Jewish. And if you talk to them, a single gesture proves that they could never be anything else. And so the years passed. During the High Holidays, they visited the Yellows, then, in the spring, they dashed over to the Greens, afterward stopping in at the Reds. After the Blacks, they visited the Whites, the sad Black family. And in the end, they put into port with the Blues. Poor Herr Blau, the mother would say, upon arriving home. Why 'poor'?—Frau Blau seemed very content. I see no reason to feel sorry for them, muttered the father, just to contradict his wife. 'Because they're so transparent, like the sky. They're everywhere, but at home nowhere,' answered Julie. 'After all, they're only Jews,' Hermann answered. 'And what about you, Hermann?' Julie retorted, something Hermann never liked. 'I am Kafka,' he said, raising his arms and letting them fall heavily a few times, his signal that, as far as he was concerned, the debate was over.

The Married Couple, Snow

It was a cold late autumn evening. A heavy, cumbersome curtain was lowered down onto the streets, catching on the tip of every branch, creased and swirling, turned up here and there by the wind. A knitted lace curtain, a heavy brocade swept along the cobblestoned street; its back arched like an emaciated cat, mangled fur standing up in all directions. Everything was threadbare. The fleeting autumn was like a beaten dog sniffing around, approaching everything suspiciously, running away and whimpering, tail between its legs, at the slightest alarming sign. So defenceless was this autumn. The wind beat against the windows. Wooden shutters opened and closed. The gas lamps covered the walls of the houses with opalescent light, the trees bereft of foliage, the shrubs. A married couple walked along the otherwise deserted and shabby street which seemed more like an underpass within a dark eddying: above, tree branches leant in towards each other, creating a strange vault in the night. Everyone who saw them would have said they were a married couple—that is why we too say they were a married couple—because in reality they were. A married couple who, apart from time spent together, apart from the ceremony prescribed by law, were also connected by an invisible bond. As they walked along the street, clinging to each other, no one could have realized nor considered that this pair, slowly drifting and moving along, the hems of their clothes turned up by the wind, had just now reached the ground, falling to the street from the whirling snow clouds above. So short was their life as they reached the end of the street built into the side of a steeply sloping hill. A child's face looked out, frightened, from one of the windows, terror-stricken at seeing the silent pair intimately leaning towards each other, their shoulders touching and then moving away. Their faces seemed blurred. The child hurried over to the window, made blurry by the vapour on the inside; on the outside, flowers of frostwork had formed on the thin glass. When, however, the child's small finger wiped off a small spot to observe more closely this pair never seen here before, they'd already moved on. They glided away as if floating on sleighs, or they drifted, the wind nudging them a bit over here, then there. Strangely, it was as if they weren't even walking—their movements gave that impression to everyone who saw them in the early twilight. They left behind no vestige. As to whether there might remain any trace on this earth of two snowflakes that meet—that is truly a question that makes you think.

Kafka's Fortieth Birthday

Every figure I have met while putting pen to paper—as with the protagonists of my own writings—wandered into the void; I tried to lead them out. I failed, though, unable to show the way out to anyone, least of all to myself; I accompanied them, wanting to open a path in that labyrinth where I came upon my poor protagonists so I could lose my way with them. I haven't been any use to them, though, because I ended up losing my own self, I blurred the way back, trampling so much in the snow that even my own left-behind footprints couldn't help me. Forty years of wandering in the plains or the desert would have been more useful: at the end, there still was admittance to the promised land. But what can I promise to those who look into my troubled writings, beyond a shame that I cannot erase—as if an offence has not occurred for which forgiveness cannot be asked.

Kafka and the Bicycle

When Kafka was a law student, and his family was still living in the apartment building known as 'Zu den drei Königen', in his room of military simplicity, the window of which looked out onto the busy street, there was—in addition to the bed, a table, a shelf filled with law books tasting of sawdust—a bicycle in the corner. His father had long resisted the idea of Franz spending his pocket money on this new contraption—superfluous, in his opinion, as well as ungainly. In discussions with his son, Hermann pronounced the invention as needless, the product of freakish minds that could only create trouble between people. No doubt, he said, it was the liberals who came up with this, along with the Freemasons, they're always wracking their brains to come up with some new world order. The old one was good enough: if it's been working so far, why can't it keep on working, Hermann grumbled. But it's the liberals who want to stop the disenfranchisement of the Jews, you should support them if for no other reason than that, Papa. Hermann didn't agree: competition meant that the best merchants kept their heads above water. The Jews are the best because they have to accomplish twice as much as everyone else. If it wasn't for that, if they weren't considered pariahs, then they wouldn't be the best any more. And if all this comes to an end, it won't lead to anything good, you'll see for yourself. The Jews will remain one people only as long they aren't allowed to live like everyone else, Hermann pronounced as if giving a speech, his voice getting louder, drowning out Franz's quiet, throttled, intentionally restrained tones. Franz used all his newfound knowledge, acquired at the law faculty, to debate with his father, and as he managed to remain patient, he hoped he'd be able to make his father quickly back down.

Hermann's final argument, when Franz almost had him forced into a corner, was to say: No matter how I look at it, this is not a Jewish thing. It was surprising to hear a statement like this—random, not based on logical principle, in no way ensuing from their previous discussion—especially from Hermann, as his own denominational affiliation, otherwise of little significance to him, had never guided his opinion before when pronouncing a judgement on this or any other new invention. He thought of it because this was a principle often invoked by the rabbis, Hermann noted, hastening to add that there was nothing about this in the Torah, either. Man goes as he is created, on foot. But if this is somehow beneath his dignity, then best he go by horse or donkey. Or by a horse-drawn tram, he added, but here he stopped, biting off the sentence, because that would lead to other possibilities, such as trains and boats—and hardly a week went by without the newspapers reporting on some kind of new flying machine. Hermann suddenly felt he was treading on troubled, and for him, uncertain ground: his son could quickly emerge victorious, defeating him when the arguments he used to counter Franz's enthusiastic words ran out. Franz, when he realized that the mere mention of the bicycle vexed his father, began to insist on it obstinately. Moreover, just to hurry things along, he picked out a random advertisement for bicycling lessons given by an experienced and trustworthy instructor. Franz went to the given address, walking along the street; he saw the sign depicting a lady leaning on her bicycle invitingly and coquettishly from far away. She wore a light bicycling costume: an aid to bodily movement which prevented overheating, allowed the free expansion of the lungs, preserving dignity and propriety for cyclists even while in motion. Franz was captivated by the elegance with which ladies and gentlemen glided along on these graceful metal structures. By this time, Franz had not spoken directly to Hermann for a long time: after the disappointments of childhood, young Franz and Hermann substituted it with the appearance of indirectness.

Why does Father object to me trying out a bicycle when most of my classmates have done so already? Franz posed the question at the dinner table to Julie sitting to his left; his upper body turned towards her, he used this pretext to remain outside Hermann's field of vision to his right. Hermann didn't look at his son who'd been vexing his father like this for a while now, after Hermann lost his self-control at one of his provocations: he began hurling ugly insults at Franz whose earlier serenity and good mood were destroyed by this overly crude and, for him, inescapable, attack; Franz sat stiff and unmoving for a long time, staring at the table. Visibly he needed time to pull himself together, not to cry as had happened so many times in his childhood. And he didn't cry, but only spoke softly to Julie, saying that certainly, my father deserves a better son than me, but perhaps this is not the fault of the son, but the mother. With that, he put his napkin down, and left the table, his back caving in. Now too he posed the question—clearly meant for Hermann—to his mother. Following custom, the father looked above him and replied to Julie, as if Franz weren't even there.

Bicycles aren't for Jews, in my opinion there's nothing to debate, but if the young lord sees things differently, let him do as he wishes and go his own way. Who cares what the father, the idiotic, uneducated rag-and-bone man has to say? As if I didn't even exist. Don't bother worrying about my opinion. Let the young university gentleman, the future Doctor of Law, do the same as his classmates, running to them and leaving family matters behind. I've seen him with those weaklings, those fine gentlemen, there's hardly a Jew among them. Still, those Jews are more like Christian converts playing at being gentlemen than *echte* goyim. They want to be like those young liberal gentlemen, enthusing over anything that annoys their elders, and of course the priests. But I know for a fact the rabbis are not the friends of these new-fangled mechanisms. It is not natural for man, created with two legs, to go rolling around on wheels.

My father leaves aside the obvious fact that—although not as conspicuously as on a bicycle—one also rolls on wheels in a horse-drawn tram; moreover, this is no less the situation in the most commonplace hansom cab, in which case my father might be willing to believe his own eyes if he has no wish to believe me, as he has determined in advance that everything that I do or want is perfidious, shoddy, a priori a madman's lunacy and sheer idiocy, said Franz, turning again towards his mother, as if his father was not sitting behind him to his right, as he always did.

Franz bought the bicycle anyway; he felt it was the happiest day of his life. He drew pleasure from its smell, he couldn't take his eyes off it, he looked at the bicycle from his bed as it stood leaning against the wall, modest in its chilled solitude. Franz felt like writing a poem to it, he would have liked people to see it, to put it by the window, for everyone to see he had his own bicycle. He sensed the smell of the metal, the grease used for lubricating the axles: in the shop, they told him he'd have to do so often. The chains especially had to be greased: they would start to rust if he didn't keep an eye on them. Franz sensed, with the mention of the chains, something unpleasant coming to mind, a kind of restraint emerging in his life.

He visited the bicycle salon once again because he wanted to show his father that he could learn, riding a bike wasn't so difficult. But he was cramped, stiff, and it was difficult. He was able to set off with the balance bike; he sensed the dizziness arising from the gliding momentum. But his father's words slowly seeped into his consciousness like poison, and when Hermann had lost all interest in what his son was doing, Franz saw how meaningless it was, and began to skip his bicycle lessons. The sight of the young ladies, however, with their flushed red faces, wearing their bicycle outfits, haunted him for a long time.

The Naked Hand

At times a person is completely at the mercy of the world that surrounds him: Kafka knew this precisely. Not everyone permits himself that experience when the face of things abruptly changes. It was said that in the cemetery, at midnight, everything came to life; the dead rose from the graves. This, of course—about the dead rising—wasn't true. Kafka once tried spending a night in the Old Jewish Cemetery to see if what people were so terrified of actually occurred. He arrived a few minutes after midnight, opening the creaking gate very carefully, then closing it behind himself just as carefully. He waited, his heart pounding, but nothing happened. The stones too were waiting, as was their wont. The oldest ones among them had been waiting for centuries now. The bones under the ground were on their way to the Holy Land, thought Kafka. Perhaps the oldest ones were already somewhere beneath the Mediterranean. It couldn't be too easy for them either, for the dead, the bones. The cemetery was as peaceful as an enchanted sea. The gravestones had been sinking for centuries now, one tilting this way, another that way. Whoever looked at them at night with only a bit of light looming saw no straight lines, only chaotic, crisscrossing forms. To Kafka, it was as if everything were surging in the darkness, although it seemed like that to him in daylight as well. Now, though, in this murky light, the tottering lines appeared to his eyes like shades.

Kafka did not believe in Jewish ghosts. And maybe that explained his visit to the Jewish cemetery. When he was a little boy, his father used to say at every meal that there were no such things as Jewish ghosts. How it is with the goyim is their business, he said. But he was adamant that no respectable Jew would ever come back from the dead. He'd had more than enough of the whole *mishpocha* when they were alive, he said, his mouth full; he began laughing at his own joke before anyone else did. His laughter turned into a choking cough, Hermann began to make rattling sounds, his face turned lilac. Julie jumped up, squeezed her hand into a fist and began to hit her husband on his back along the spine to dislodge the morsel stuck in his larynx. Put him out of his misery, God, suffocate him, whispered Franz to Ottla, sitting beside him; she was still too little to get the joke. She wrinkled her brows, though, to rebuke her unruly older brother. Still, there was a kind of complicity between them. Ottla wished her father no harm, and yet she watched the large body struggling, the wide shoulders' awkward convulsions, with derision. Franz was repeating a remark he'd once heard in the shop: a shop girl had said the same thing about an older shop assistant, when he too, face reddened and with terror in his eyes, began to choke. No one rushed over to strike his back. But now Julie immediately jumped up, and with a practised hand, freed the morsel that Hermann had wolfed down, ending up in the wrong place.

Hermann did not say thank you, he only became ill-tempered, and yelled at his son: You're still laughing at your father? he asked, his voice rattling stertorously; not waiting for a reply, he continued eating more quietly. The roast goose was dripping with grease; around Hermann's mouth, his protruding chin glistened, the grease smeared everywhere. Smaller shreds of roast goose dangled from the corner of his mouth, Franz noticed as he turned to his father. He didn't answer his question: he had not been called upon to answer it, and so could not. Hermann threw the goose bones underneath the table out of vexation: the small plate which he had to pretend to use because of Julia hadn't been placed on the table. He couldn't follow his natural inclination of getting rid of the bones, as he'd done in the old days, before Julie had forbidden him: more precisely, she had once cautiously remarked that this was not the custom in the Löwy household, even if it was what he did at home; she enjoined him to refrain from such behaviour when lunching with her parents. From this remark, Hermann understood that this expectation, cautiously pronounced by his spouse, had originated with Julie's family. Hermann immediately left the table, but as he respected his wife—she was, after all, his business partner who'd brought the initial capital to the marriage, always standing beside him with wise counsel and family connections, helping him to run the business and manage the household—he took her words into consideration. A few days later, he requested a small plate for the bones: Julie still had not dared to place one next to him herself, as was the custom in her parents' house, lest Hermann take offence, as he did with so many other things.

Kafka on the Bridge

It was already evening when this story began. The light of the arc lamps turned the thick fog into a woolly substance. The lamplight struggled, flickering disconsolately. It was as if there wasn't enough air, or as if it had been confined to an unbearably small space and couldn't wait to break free. A dark, tall, ridiculously gaunt man was looking at the water. Seeing him from afar, leaning over the stone balustrade, one might have thought that he had dropped something into the river and now was searching for it, looking amid the fugitive waves sweeping along branches or other objects of uncertain, hard-to-define shape. Kafka, however, was not watching the water, but himself; as he had been doing so often recently, he was thinking of suicide. There were still gas lamps in some places where there hadn't been enough money to replace them, the manes of the stone lions on Charles Bridge seemed to flutter in this light. Of course, they were all motionless and cold, rigid as statues must be. Their naked skin was smooth. In some spots, where the passers-by caressed them, they shone as if wet with perspiration. Only the naked skin of the passers-by was traversed by goosebumps when touched. The lions watched the waters of the Moldau indifferently, its surface rippling around the pillars and depicting changing patterns: there was always something to watch. Kafka was preparing for a trip, immersed in his thoughts. He had come down from Goldenes Gäßchen, from Hradschin, and, as he crossed the bridge, he looked at the water. The fleeting thought crossed his mind that this water could rush onward with him, too, if he were to throw himself over the balustrade, if he were to entrust himself to this river, to the quiet and humble Moldau he'd known ever since childhood. But did the river know him? the thought crossed his mind. Perhaps this river was a true god, a kind of spirit that existed and remembered, as did every other entity that changed over the course of time. He imagined the Moldau sweeping along this ridiculous body that was his own; all of his cares—stemming from his inability to make peace with this body—would finally come to an end, this body that was precisely the means by which he could make his own self visible to others, something inconceivable in its absence. He couldn't ask—he could never ask Felice—to forget his exterior, to forget all that was contingent beyond himself, to concentrate on the essential things, to regard him as he was: a hand that wrote to her unceasingly, then folded up the paper and placed it in an envelope. If you folded an envelope like that you could also make a paper boat, an impulse that Kafka felt strongly at times: to send the pages covered with his writing floating down the Moldau. The water would slowly read his scribbling, those shameful signs that Kafka had put down on the pages. To obliterate the traces of his ignominious life: everything that had occurred in the past few days now urged him to do this. Next year in Jerusalem as they said, but nothing would ever come from the trip he had planned with Felice and Max to Palestine.

Conversation at the Table

Well, those Jews, you know they're crazy. I'm telling you, not even one of them is normal, said Kafka, confidently referring to his business associates at the dinner table, ever louder and more insistent after the third glass of wine. Then he began recounting specific incidents, jumping from one to the other, insatiably absorbed in the joy of the telling: how the others were so much worse than him, how he was so much better than his associates and friends whom otherwise he was really quite fond of, to whom his survival was so closely connected, to his life, through him to his family's, and of course to Anselm's life as well. But he never spoke of these associates and friends with recognition, at the very most with a kind of indulgence. Love is not recognition, at the very most it is acceptance, in the worst case forbearance, endurance for the sake of love, as the Protestant goyim put it. He was speaking to his wife, but the children were there as well: Anselm also heard what Blau and Grün, Schwarz and Gelb, Roth and Weiß had said and done that day at the market.

130

More precisely, Anselm K. didn't understand anything in relation to 'the business', he wasn't even drawn to this 'business' where only the only one who could ever emerge victorious was Father, and others were attributed meaning only in relation to him. The children have to learn how to trade. There's nothing base about it, Father had said so many times to Mother: an advantageous contract is no sin, no trickery, but simply a favourable deal set down on paper. Does a man have the right to cut down the branch he's sitting on? Of course he does, I'm telling you, he repeated after some time, especially if he had already emptied the second glass, and he was a bit tipsy from the kosher brandy kept in the credenza for the holidays.

Otherwise, things always go around in a circle, he liked to reiterate, as a way of assuaging his own conscience. Your profit is someone else's loss, but tomorrow brings the turn of the dice, and Adonai will pay back the one you took from today. If He doesn't pay him back through you, He'll use another who has the means. The main thing is that everyone is part of a system in which the chances and possibilities are distributed unevenly. Why should I get all sentimental if someone else is deluged with plans and opportunities but doesn't know what to do with them? These Jews, he said—because Hermann's business associates were almost exclusively Jewish—they're all crazy, do you hear me? And the names they run around with all day, so excited, as if the Messiah were getting ready to come to Prague, and they have to arrange their affairs before the evening candle lighting, because who knows how much time they'll have afterward if the Messiah is already here. And what will happen to time as such—wondered

Anselm K., but of course only later, when he was writing it all down—as long as we're on the subject, Hermann, namely, the father, continued. Just think about it, they'll be speculating that the word 'time' doesn't mean anything any more: time was only created to make space to wait for the coming of the Messiah, so that we'd have something to call it, so it could have some kind of dimension, no matter how small. Of course, I don't know what the rabbis or the university professors would have to say about this, but I'm convinced that if people hadn't invented time—the idea that so much time has passed and so much time will pass from a certain day onward—in brief, if this continual speculation between labour and available time had never been invented, then money itself never would have been invented. Which of course would have been good, because then there wouldn't be this situation where one has a lot and the other has little—that's obvious, no?—and yet it would also be bad, because there would be no way to purchase other people's time so that we can get rich. Still, one person would have as much time as the next: everyone would get the same twelve hours in one day, which is exactly enough time for the day to come to an end but still not enough for the day's work to get done. To take one example: yesterday I received a delivery, but it would have taken me a solid week to load it all into the warehouse, so I purchased the time of nine people, and by that evening everything was warehoused. The only problem is that I can't buy even more time, I still have to close up shop at five in the evening, just like my neighbour there Blau, although what a lousy little joint he runs. Of course, during the same opening hours I could run two or three other shops with two or three times the inventory, assistants and apprentices, and

if I had lots of customers, I could offer—of course only very discreetly, only to regular customers—smaller or larger discounts if
they stopped shopping at Blau's; but as for staying open for eight
hours, that's prescribed by law. Because if Blau didn't have his
shop, then I wouldn't have to purchase more time, namely, everyone, during those same eight hours, would come to my shop. And
finally, if I bought out Blau, it would be the same as if I were
buying time . . .

These and other such orations were Father's way of thinking
out loud. As Anselm K. noted it all down later on, he was aston-
ished to realize that his father—who bore the fearful name of
Hermann, who from the outside appeared in no way Jewish,
dressed in well-tailored suits, the fabric tightly stretched against
the hard musculature of his soldier-like bearing, his face always
meticulously shaved, using the same soap and fragrances as the
other city merchants, and imitating, precisely in everything, the
behaviour of government functionaries and genteel goy shop-
keepers—that there was nothing Jewish about his father at all.
Missing most of all from Hermann's words was that quality of
speculation, the continual variability: well, if we look at it this
way, then we can say yes, but looking at it from another way, then
we would say no. That never-ending deliberation of words, that
pondering, semantic hair-splitting: here is a shade of meaning that
we have not yet fully understood, but which somehow must be
unravelled from the words. Missing from Hermann was even the
slightest trace of this unflagging and, at its base, aimless cogitation.
When he spoke, Hermann used speech as a tool of command, like
a soldier or anyone else in uniform, someone whom Anselm K.
might have encountered in the city. Put this here, put that there.

This is what he always heard from Hermann when sometimes he, namely, his father, took Anselm into the shop, mentioned at home only in tones of devotion. In the shop, everyone was goy, even though half of Hermann's staff was Jewish: the other half were people who didn't look like Jews, because they weren't. Of course, Hermann demanded that the Jews he employed not look like Jews: no ear locks, no bowing, no reminders in these genteel surroundings of despised Jewish customs. But he also didn't mind if one of his employees suddenly revealed their Jewishness, he even encouraged them to call out 'Shalom' after the departing customers, it was fine with him. Even if they immediately corrected themselves with *Auf wiedersehen* or *Dobrý den*. Because then the customer, if he himself wasn't Jewish, could think to himself: Well, these Jews, they can be decent after all. And if the customer was a Jew who didn't want to look like one, then he could be happy about the shared complicit wink with the shop assistant; or, if he was the kind of Jew who wanted to look like a Jew—although that kind hardly ever set foot in Hermann's fancy shop—he could also be happy, thinking *ja gut*, that was a decent Jew, only that . . . And here the customer was lost in his thoughts, speculating at length within himself, and given half the chance, he would do the same with others as well, all day and night, or until both of them got exhausted as one could never manage to convince the other . . . Well, this got on Hermann's nerves, these Jews couldn't even let themselves be persuaded of something, so why did they stand around conjecturing about everything? Not one of them was capable of insight, they only liked to while away the time, this surmising, splitting apart words, well, what they liked was exactly what he hated and despised with his entire heart. Just as he despised those Jews who could not—for millennia now—rid themselves of their unpleasant customs, just like his father, Hermann said, his father whom he hated, because he was his father and he had begot innumerable children, but he was not able to take care of even one of them, he never give them enough so that their stomachs would stop growling for at least a moment, said Hermann. Not like it is for all of you—and he triumphantly looked at his family, above the richly laid table, at the cowed children spooning their soup with bent heads, and he looked at his wife, this diminutive creature who lived in Hermann's shadow with his enormous physique; perhaps that was why she was so pale.

If Hermann was not giving commands when he spoke, then he was simply deciding on something, his verdict unquestionable and definitive. Speech, for him, signified decision: I'm buying this now, I'll pay this much. Or: Take your things and leave right away, you're fired, I don't need an assistant who can't persuade our customers that what happened at that shoddy Blau's could never happen here. Or, while he was picking his teeth, he would, with slurred speech, once again list his business adversaries whom, as a closing to the meal, he vilified, his judgement was immediate as he pronounced, irrevocably: Schwarz was a cheater, Roth was a hypocrite, Katzmarek a pederast. Anselm Kafka did not know the meaning of 'pederast'.

Over the course of time, Anselm K. realized—as he wrote this all down in his unwieldy diaries, in his letters; every untouched piece of paper was an available surface for him, by night and by day, instead of sleeping he just wrote and wrote—he realized, while he wrote, that for Hermann, every long and repetitive speech given at family meals constituted that very Jewish custom for which, otherwise, Hermann had so much contempt, as he mentioned at times in regard to his own father. Otherwise, Anselm K. knew hardly anything about Hermann's father: the only point of commonality was that this father appeared to be his grandfather, but Hermann hardly ever spoke about him, only occasionally and disdainfully, as a deterrent example, an alarming case of futile quibbling, meaningless speculation and unreal brooding. With his figure, Hermann wanted to dissuade Anselm from this kind of repugnant—if not to say, Jewish—behaviour, from which God protected his family: namely, that he, the Father, was, fortunately, already protected, and now he must pray and do everything in his power lest this disease raise its head in his family; first and foremost, he must protect his son and he must use fear, if there were no other means, to keep him from this virulent contagion. Anselm K., however, received the antitoxin, cast into words, in such enormous quantities and doses during his child-hood, youth, and—due to unfortunate circumstances—his adulthood as well, that the antitoxin was transformed into a toxin: he began to feel evermore interest in his grandfather, and instead of being alarmed, was drawn more and more to this 'Jewish behav-iour'. Hermann's deep antipathy for the Jews, as Anselm K. was to suspect later on, was presumably caused by Hermann's own suspicion as to whether his eponymous father was his genetic one. Was there not some concealed and secretive distance between the name and that which the name designated: the name of the father, K., and his body, which bore the name of K. but who had entered the world via his mother—therefore only the mother was certain, and perhaps this suspicion had ensconced itself somewhere in Hermann's unuttered thoughts, as Anselm noted down in his diaries in which he wrote nearly unceasingly. Namely, Anselm compulsively registered, through writing, the world around him, and as he always felt himself a slightly foolish and simple child, incapable of meeting the adult world on its own terms, he hoped, through writing, to comprehend all the obscure and incomprehensible things happening around him. Anselm never thought about, and certainly would have refuted the hypothetical parallel between his own maniacal habit and Hermann's rambling dinner-table lectures (fully alien to his resolute and, it could be said, extremely rational nature)—that between these two things, there might exist a secretive and inner bond. This bond was the antipathy towards Jewish behaviour and its disguised concession. Just as, for Hermann, speech was something beyond things, and otherwise a deeply scorned conjecture, Anselm K. used his maniacal need to write to create a connection between himself and the surrounding world. Part of this world was the dead father, who, like a dybbuk, the returning spirit of the dead, was still present, and spoke to Anselm directly, demanding an explanation from him for everything that Hermann would have liked to demand of his own father. Once again you're late, once again, as always, you went to bed too late. You're always just scratching out those daft lines of yours, even though I asked you to go to sleep early, because today I'm going to need you in the shop.

The Fart

We see Kafka as he crosses the Old Town Square, the cobblestones delineated like a raster pattern. It could be afternoon, an autumn afternoon. To be completely precise, late autumn. The lights are sharp, the air crystal clear, as if there were a breeze. The Old Town Square is like a photograph traversed by Herr Doctor, as he is addressed in the office. His lanky frame totters in the wind. He buttons his coat up carefully so that his chest, more precisely the lungs positioned anatomically and regularly inside his chest, will be protected.

'Franz, button up your coat,' Hermann called after him that morning, his thoughts already preoccupied with the business. He's dissatisfied with the assistants, dissatisfied, although he's still at home. When he steps into the shop, the tittering stops at the sound of the small bell tinkling above the door, but no one dares look in his direction. The employees withstand his invective silently. Behind Hermann's words—'Franz, button up your coat'—this invective already lay. It scorches like embers. Franz now senses that his coat is buttoned too tightly. It burns his throat.

It's as if the wind today wasn't so sharp, he thinks, as it was this morning when he walked to the office.

'Good morning, Herr Doctor,' the porter greets him, clicking his heels together, his uniform tightly buttoned, the fabric stretched across his potbelly. The Insurance Company postal clerk is Czech but, out of sheer courteousness, he always greets Kafka in German. Franz replies in Czech, out of obliging attentiveness. Then the porter inquires in Czech after the health of Herr Doctor. Franz bats the question away with a joke, and yet perhaps only he detects what lies beneath it: namely, if Herr Doctor is ill—as he has deigned to state for years now, sojourning for ever-longer periods of time in sanatoria, never neglecting to mail lovely postcards with pictures of mountains, sending his greetings to the porter as well—then why not take retirement already? The unstated question can be heard in the porter's query, as he—and everyone else in the office—knows that the family of Herr Doctor enjoys, let us say, a certain material basis. Inasmuch as Herr Doctor surely would not wish to further subject his unstable health to the travails of taxing office duties, this family background, including the recent establishment of a new factory of great promise would—to put it briefly—certainly guarantee the ailing Herr Doctor a sufficient basis for quiet contemplation.

'You must spare yourself, Herr Doctor. And a scarf wouldn't hurt in this miserable weather,' the porter adds, whereupon Franz senses that the porter is trying for a certain over-familiarity—perhaps due to his own carelessness, as he has transgressed the set time limit, observed by all his colleagues, for conversation with him. He tries to close the conversation, on the verge of breaching the established order of office communication, quickly.

'My father insists that I wear a coat and do up all the buttons. Although as far as I'm concerned, it isn't so cold as to necessitate the wearing of a cloak. Chiefly, I consider doing up the buttons of one's coat all the way up to the neck as a premature and unduly hasty measure,' Franz continues. 'A premature and unduly hasty measure': what exquisite sophistry for a conversation like this, Franz writes that evening in his diary, I command no authority; I have my scrawny physique to thank for that. A moustached ruddy-cheeked fellow with a beer belly disconcerts me immediately.

The porter chases away the Insurance Company clients in Czech. He nails the obstinate and hopeless cases, subjects them to brief interrogations, not letting them past. With this mysterious capability of his, the porter has made himself indispensable in the Office. The management spoils him because he represents enormous savings for them. Does the porter only know how to say hello in German, or is it possible he understands everything?—this thought crosses Franz's mind. Why wouldn't be it possible, Franz trundles the question further on within himself. He's thinking about this as he stands in front of the porter, hesitating as to whether he should move on or stand here for a bit, offering his solidarity even wordlessly. Maybe he should say something to this person who always clicks his heels in such a soldier-like manner, his bearing humble and respectful, which makes Franz feel afraid. What do the others say at times like this, he asks himself, and perhaps he's even thinking that he forgot to observe his colleagues secretly to see how they behave at times like this.

'That coat suits Herr Doctor very well, and undoubtedly is highly serviceable in such weather as this.'

This man obviously used to be a soldier, perhaps the fleeting thought occurs to Franz. He was one of that kind. Men like that are all the same. Kafka knows well that such jobs, confidential positions, as they are called, comfortable, gentlemanly, necessitating contact with the common folk on a daily basis, could only be had in exchange for a service. You have to earn it. It means entering the service of the existing order, its unjust and ruthless mechanisms, renouncing one's personal opinions and feelings, what philosophers like to term the self. That world whose key is the self may never be opened again, thought Franz. The porter is a good man, he noted that evening in his diary—he has heard this statement from a few complainants, who, through error, a moment of vacillation on the part of the porter, or perhaps a bribe, have—very infrequently—made their way up to his office. The porter is a good man, he's one of us, he knows life, say those who previously were sent away many times by the porter whose voice at such times is calm but severe. They receive his words as if a judgement, silently, heads bent, the widows look at the tips of their shoes, the elderly fathers who have lost their grown sons. The porter knows life, he doesn't mean us ill, it's only that we can't resign ourselves, they say.

Franz is afraid of the porter, he would like to be free of him. The porter senses this as well: he tries to extend the moment a bit to take further enjoyment in Herr Doctor's confusion. Now too, as always, his boots are polished, shining without blemish. His belt is also shining, it glistens blackly. His face is also shiny in the sunlight falling upon it. It is taut and ruddy like an apple. There's a shiny layer on the apple as well, some kind of waxy, greasy, sticky material. Franz doesn't like to have any physical contact with him, he doesn't even like shaking his hand, the thought of having to pull off his glove fills him with dread. If he has to shake hands with the porter, he runs to his office immediately, splashing water from the jug into the handwashing basin; he soaps his moist skin thoroughly and at length. And yet, for some unclear reason, he would like to touch him. He has become interested in the origin of the shining surface on apples and on the porter's face.

Is it really sticky? he posed the question to himself. But he didn't dare touch him. When he considered the question more deeply, he hardly even dared think about it.

The porter never has never stated or referred to the fact that he knows who Franz is. But when he speaks to Franz in German, pronouncing a greeting and a few polite inquiries after his health, his manner is always slightly peculiar, just as it is now with Franz standing in front of him, his posture peculiar and birdlike, head hanging down at the end of his gaunt figure, bent forward, dangling in the porter's direction. The porter is a small, thickset man with the inclination to corpulence customary of men who substitute the joys of women and bed with those of the table, namely, food. From that point on, flesh is interesting for such porters only in its boiled or roasted forms. They long for the table surrounded by friends, they endure, with a light heart, the discomforts of the restaurant's folding summer chairs, drawn only by the pints of beer with its head of foam, packed in ice, the joy of golden nectar poured into sparkling glasses. The smell of beer remains on the bottom of the moustache the entire day, and we can see the hardened foam on the matted strands hanging down.

Franz recalls a picture, a picture from memory, when, in honour of the Emperor's birthday, the office was open for only half the day, and the employees of the Insurance Company went to a nearby beer house. Franz didn't wish to go, but his reluctance was starting to become both suspicious and inconvenient: it could have been interpreted as disrespect towards the directors of the Company or even the Emperor himself.

Franz's father never endured disrespect of any sort, he always retaliated immediately. In the beginning, it was with beatings; later on, when Franz had grown taller, and wore long trousers instead of short ones, his girlish voice replaced by one that reverberated, cawing and breaking, his smooth and soft skin now covered with abominable bumps and abscesses, squeezed out, scratched, and oozing, his nose having grown longer, and the entire head seemingly suggesting some newer birth defect, from that point on, his father—who knew why, maybe from revulsion—never raised a hand to him again. Certainly, this is how his father behaved with him, thought Franz, as he presumed no deviation from how his own father had been treated growing up.

When Franz was already a grown man, now taller than his father, and Hermann, getting older and older, seemed much shorter than Franz, who was suddenly much taller, he became, surprisingly, something like one of Franz's old childhood toys, Franz noted once in his diary. My old battered teddy bear, says Franz as he walks alongside him, that's exactly what he's like: his coat is dusty and his shoes squeak, the way they slip on the cobblestones make a sound just like the creaking straw stuffed in his old teddy bear. And, as is often common after a certain age, Franz hears his father fart protractedly, as he walks. It's in rhythm with his shift of balance as he walks, from the right leg to the left, then resting a bit, then conversely, from the left to the right, with a few moments pause in between. It's if a bagpipe were strolling in the Old City, across Wenzelsplatz. At times the weight of the body rests a bit on one leg. Then it doesn't all come out. Then it stiffens a bit and the gases escape, the opposite shoulder sinks down. The body of the father is like that old teddy bear who he used to call Bubu, sometimes he called it my son, and on festive occasions, at the time of the autumn holidays, he called it my Kaddish. After several glasses of wine. Franz got the teddy bear from him as well.

'I don't know' he said, 'what good it is to play with dolls, a proper Jewish child doesn't do that and doesn't build nativity scenes either, but your mother said that you wanted this the most of all. Here, take this,' he said, and he pressed the hatbox into Franz's hands: tied up with coloured ribbon, one of Hermann's employees might have placed the old-fashioned teddy bear inside.

The Case

My name is Franz Kafka, he said. That is to say, I am called Franz Kafka, he immediately corrected himself. But this is of no significance from the perspective of the *case*. I do not wish to detail the particulars of why such a differentiation is required. From your point of view, my name merely signifies that of a solicitor appointed to your case. I do not represent you who stands in litigious relation with our institution, and the adjudication of this matter does not pertain to me. I can do nothing to further the interest of your case in terms of either an advantageous or disadvantageous outcome. It is not me with whom you speak, but a solicitor who, utilizing the legal instruments at his disposal within the realm of possibility, impartially endeavours—you may rest assured—to set forth, to those entities who shall ultimately render a decision, all pertinent circumstances in as detailed a fashion as possible. However, it is much more difficult than you might think to choose, from the extenuating circumstances, those most relevant to the judgement at hand. We can never know—when someone, or some people, are to render a decision—which circumstances, however seemingly trifling and insignificant, will be accorded significance by them later on.

I will tell you, at this point, a story. But before I begin, I would like to call your attention to the fact that you should really pay attention. This is not your story. Namely, the story, as once someone [ ]—and here, he made a strange movement, as it were gesturing to the far distance behind his back—must be told in such a way that people will be helped.

My dear son,

I don't say that it's hard to be a father, because every father wants to leave a son behind. I won't forget the pride I felt when you were born. And yet how little merit was there of mine in this. I gave thanks for you to God, I praised you in the temple. 'My son was born. The firstborn son. This is how it must be.' And I even believed I was clever. Of course, it's a deal: one out of two. Either a boy or a girl. You can't really go wrong. And you weren't a girl, but a boy. And that was something, so I intervened in the business. I always had a good hand for it, I believed that for a long time. And when you were born, I had no doubts. I succeeded at everything. A boy was living proof: God loves me. He gave me a son. For us Jews, this is particularly important, as you yourself are aware. But you don't want a son, I know. Because he would remind you of me. My father wanted a son so he could say so in the temple. If you had a son, you wouldn't praise him. And especially not in the temple. I know you wouldn't know what to do with him. Maybe it's good you never had a son. That wouldn't be good, I see that now. Not for you, and certainly not for the child.

It's hard to be a father, because a father is not always lucky as a mother who carries her son for nine months beneath her heart. If I'd had the chance to do that, then I think I would have had enough time to get used to how difficult a child is, especially if it's a boy. Because a boy will make the father think of death most of all. Of the path he has tread until now. Of the things he never did. The women that he left. Although you don't like to hear this. I recall how you were offended once when I was speaking about how a man has to learn how to leave women. How to deceive them—use them. And never be overcome by your conscience, because then you're done for. Women's tears, their despondency is a form of theatre, their way of trapping men. You spoke once, my son, of the song of the sirens. I never went to Gymnasium, I don't know about these things. But I understood that the sirens live in the bodies of women.

I used to see, in childhood, how the tomcats would strangle the kittens, if they found them. The female cats would hide their young. I never understood why, if the mother wasn't there, they didn't find all of these rheumy new-born kittens. There was certainly no problem with their sense of smell. There must have been some reason why they didn't kill all of them. If every male kitten were destroyed as a helpless suckling, then the species would die out. Somehow they know this, that's why they don't do it. The rabbis would certainly know the answer. They just beat around the bush, though, until they finally pull something out of the Talmud or the Torah. Although what can our God have in common with these new-born kittens? Well, never mind.

Although animals as repulsive as that are few. And people even say they're clean. Because it digs a little hole when it poops. The mother teaches her kittens to poop, so that, after suckling, when the time comes, she licks their little bottoms, preparing them to poop. It wouldn't occur to them otherwise, or they squeeze their rectum so tightly, that they can only loosen their muscles like that, who knows. Phooey, what an unclean species.

Your life is my death, I see this. Although you have said that is because of me that you cannot live. That I take the air away from you. That I am such a big, confident, strong, cheerful and large-statured man—I am what you'd have to be for me to be satisfied with you. But as you will never be anything like that, I cannot take any pleasure in you. And as you will never be that which you should become, your life is meaningless. And for all this, you make me responsible. And yet you parasite off me, you live off me, your writings speak of me as well. Without me, you wouldn't be able to write about anything, which, as you say, is the most important thing for you.

As I did not do what the tomcats did, I did not strike you down when you were little, I can no longer hurt you. I think that by now only you can hurt me, by attributing all of your failures to me. And finally, you do so by leaving me alone in my old age, and making my shame complete, so that I will have to say the Kaddish for you now, and not vice versa. Therefore, I can only beg you for mercy, as in your eyes I lost all my authority long ago, and since you too are a grown man now, I see no difference whatsoever.

The Civil Servant

'At first glance, I look like a civil servant,' Kafka says to the young man, then he quickly corrects himself: 'At first glance, one takes me to be a civil servant,' he reformulates the sentence, although civil servants usually button up their coats, he added that evening in his diary, their belts pulled tightly around their waists, and they couldn't exist without their elbow patches and sleeve guards, because a true civil servant is unimaginable without these accessories. The natural number of the civil servant is the plural, that is mainly what they use. In the singular, this word is so orphaned and uncustomary. We are a straitened and closed class, the reserve division of bourgeois society, he adds, bearing the correct attitude of sharp professionalism. The militant spirit is that of patriotism, he repeats the slogan emphasized so often by Herr Director, a thought which he, Kafka, does not share, as neither the militant nor the patriotic spirit suits him—he reminds himself by repeating this sentence. 'In the Office, the expression *I* is to be avoided: in official language, it is considered an inexcusable error of style. The *I*, just as the deed and existence itself, is invoked to serve a grammatical time that no longer exists.'

'Herr Kafka,' the Director said to him recently, rolling with pleasure the *r*'s in the word *Herr*. Well, Herr Kafka, he took another stab at addressing him, repeating that detested letter *r*, deliberately and warningly using the word *Herr* instead of *pan*, designating, with scornful emphasis, that Kafka—that is to say, myself, the civil servant noted that night in his diary, do not belong among those whom the new spirit, the new state, the new nation view with pleasure. 'Herr Kafka may not speak with the clients in such a way, employing such terms as "I think that . . . " and "it is my opinion that . . . " and other such imprecise flippancies. The accurate phrasing will use the first-person plural or the general subject, in which either *we* or the *Office* will be the subject of the sentence. This use of the first-person singular must be discarded. It does not and never did exist, it was never customary, or perhaps during the slovenliness of that accursed monarchy, among those persons communicating in Prague German dialect'—the director interjected this subtly genteel anti-Semitic remark—'as they could allow themselves to do so,' here, he held a pause for effect and took a deep breath. 'Still,' he continued, 'it is possible, that Herr Kafka has overheard such expressions or saw them being written down, but now there is a fresh breeze blowing through the land. And whoever is displeased, is unpleased,' the director finished his speech with a certain incongruity of style, if he was even aware of the Germanism—Kafka muttered to himself thinking back and remembering the incident from weeks before. 'Then, a bitter smile runs across the man's face: we shall bequeath our body to our sons in the spirit of ledger entries and values carried: our sons, who themselves will be civil servants, in the service of the nation and the common good. The smile plays around his lips which he squeezes together tightly, and the resulting lock is like the line of a blade, so tightly are his lips pressed together due to an inner tension which might be the sign of bodily fatigue or disquiet of the soul. Accuracy and trustworthiness are the greatest values of the civil servant who does not ask questions but only carries out the assignment at hand,' he mutters, while the wind unpredictably tugs and pulls at his cloak, customarily worn by the civil-servant corps as well as postmen and railway men, a garment maligned as the 'piglet-snatcher'. In the time of the Monarchy, all postmen, railway men and civil servants of Central Europe wore such pelerines, cloaks and 'piglet-snatchers'—he recalls this from his youth—but such cloaks were still needed in the new successor states, and as there was little hope for newer supplies, everyone donned these items of clothing with concentrated caution and circumspection. He put it on in the morning when his father warned him: It will be windy today, put on your pig-snatcher. He was not too happy to satisfy his father's demands, his father who continued to treat him like a child who had to be kept within sight. Still, he put it on, but out of stubbornness didn't button it up. Every time he glimpsed it hanging from the office coat hanger, his father's gaze was there, wordlessly, as if the coat had absorbed it and now radiated it towards him. This impeded him when, in the afternoon, as he stepped out of the Insurance Company building precisely at 5 o'clock and zero minutes, nodding at the porter stationed in his booth, who—monarchy or not—was a person of military character. Acknowledging his nod, the porter always raised his hand to his shako, as a former military man he saluted him enthusiastically; despite the wind blowing from the neighbouring street thrusting into his chest, he did not button up his pelerine to protect himself against the cold. This black cloth fluttered next to him all along the chilly, windy streets, looking something like a large bird as he tottered back to the family apartment on the Großer Ring, the thrusts of wind either quickening or slowing down his weary steps, clumsy on the ground, attempting descent: staggering, it tries to find its balance, cautiously closes its large wings, learns a suitable rhythm for walking on the earth.

He's alone, he leans forward into the wind, so strong it can hold up the light hovering weight of his body. Every evening he writes in his diary: of course, anyone who comes across him on these late autumn streets, shrouded in rushing winds, as he scratches out his restless evening stroll, would never realize that. We see a peculiar—because grotesquely gangling—and skinny figure walking down Zeltnerstraße, more recently Celetná ulice. The wind sometimes catches up the wings of his transitional-weather coat sewn from flannel. It lifts them up; the man tries to hold down the flapping, lashing cloth wings with his arms. But he doesn't button up his coat, he squeezes his walking cane tightly, he raises the leather bag carried by civil servants in front of himself with his other hand, as if protecting himself from the wind and the passers-by. I force myself across the square as if waging fierce battle with the grim forces of nature. And all the while I know that in the building across from me resides the one whose protection is served by all these forces wishing to impede my arrival. A powerful sorcerer stands there commanding the winds, forces assisting him in the protection of the house. My father stands there and directs the elements. Through his servants he directs the snowflakes falling into my eyes, the windstorm immediately arises, so that not only are diamond-edged ice particles thrust into the fissures of my eyes, but they also reach into the fissures of my coat, so that my lungs will cease to function, just as even now they bear me with difficulty. With the eyes of my soul, I see my father on the second floor.

'I know that at times like these, my father stands before the window, he is watching the square, the western . . . corner of the Großer Ring, where he is waiting for me to emerge, he writes that evening in his diary, there is anxiety and impatience in him with regards to me, as always,' he says to Milena, when they go for a walk the next day.

Well, in that case, he loves you, Milena remarks casually.

Yes, undoubtedly, as he knows how to love. I, however, know with certainty that he watches me, and that this attention [ ] me

My dear son,

This is the last letter I'm writing to you, one you won't receive, and only I will read it. For a few years now, I have suspected that this would be the end, but still I hoped it would not be me standing at your grave, but you standing at mine. If I think about it though, I always suspected it. Perhaps ever since your siblings Georg and Hermann died. Twice I have stood by a small coffin, with you by my side, if you perhaps recall, twice I had to recite the Kaddish, of which you didn't understand a word, and I myself understood only a little. But I did understand that the existence of the Almighty is the one certitude in face of which everything else is just empty talk. Words that I never had anything to do with. It was not with words that I traded, as you did, only through words. I wasn't happy about your passion, writing, that you played with words, words that belong to that being who took from me your two brothers, and finally you as well. Well, it has not been given to me for my sons to stand by my grave, and for me not to stand at the grave of my sons. I was always afraid that a curse stood upon you. And you always tortured yourself with the thought that

155

you were cursed. Now I know that the curse is upon me. And upon your mother. And that there could be no more bitter disillusionment than this. Amen.

TRANSLATOR'S AFTERWORD

In the spring of 2010, I received an email from Szilárd Borbély:

> For two years now I have been preparing something like
> a novel about Kafka with the title of *Kafka's Son*. Now,
> my duties of the semester are slowly diminishing, and I
> have begun writing; I hope I will be able to finish it. This
> topic interests me. I have a smaller or perhaps slightly
> larger request: would you happen to have any maps of
> Prague from the 1920s or 30s? I would like to get a map
> of where Kafka lived, of the city centre, if one existed,
> could you make a copy of it? Or send it as a photograph.

In response, I sent an internet link to a series of historical maps of
Prague, located on the server of the Czech Institute of Geodesy,
Topography and Cartography. The author commented that the
maps were very useful, with the one disadvantage: they could not
be printed out. However, with his usual consideration, he urged
me not to spend any money on maps or go to too much trouble
on his behalf. About a week later, he wrote that he had found two

1920s Reiseführer maps in the Debrecen university library, which he had been able to photocopy. At that time, I also sent him a copy of *Franz Kafka und Prag*, by Harold Salfellner.

It would appear that Borbély ceased work on the 'novel-like thing', as he referred to it in another email, sometime in 2010. Work on *Kafka's Son* had commenced as early as 2004, the year he published the first edition of *Final Matters*. The manuscript, as he left it at the time of his death in 2014, had a title page but was clearly 'unfinished' in the sense of its partially fragmentary nature, with occasional incomplete and unfinished sentences, notes by the author interpolated into the text, and so on. As a translator, I have not attempted to 'mend' any of these rough edges, only appending a translator's note where sentences trail off, repeat, or display inconsistencies. Whether intended or not, we can see the fragmentary state in which Borbély left *Kafka's Son* as a re-echoing of a number of Kafka's own fragmentary prose works, most notably his final novel *Amerika*.

Borbély's intense identification with Kafka is well known to his readership—Kafka was one of the central figures of his verse collection *Berlin-Hamlet*. Yet perhaps his most explicit discussion of his relationship to this author appeared in a still-unpublished essay of his, 'The World of Kafka and the Culture of Brutality'. In this piece, written in fact as part of a grant proposal, he states:

> I have been working on the first part of the project, a novel entitled *Kafka's Son*, for a number of years: the first draft of the manuscript is approaching completion but still requires a great deal of work. The novel analyses events having to do with Kafka's youth. Through the eyes

of the father, Hermann Kafka, the son, Franz Kafka, is envisioned; he in turn envisions Felice Bauer and Grete Bloch through the eyes of his own imaginary son. The gaze of the son is the gaze of fear based upon history, because it at once shows the son is the father and the father as the son, unifying the past and the future within their own selves.

This novel in part continues the themes of my collection *Berlin-Hamlet* (2003): the relationship between Felice/Ophelia and Franz/Hamlet as ultimately poisoned by a wavering search for identity. In this cycle of poems, the temporal experience of this condition is rendered lyrically: the uncertainty of identity, the erasure of its boundaries is shown to be a particular feature of certain eras of societal change and crisis. The formation of identity at such times is fraught with peril and moreover cannot be completed: the correspondence of Kafka/Hamlet, seeking Felice/Ophelia ultimately unravels the identities of both of these figures, possibly the reason for the cessation of their engagement.

The genesis of the novel *Kafka's Son* brings together personal and general interconnections in this regard. It examines the paths of thought and identity in Eastern Europe. Franz Kafka and Felice Bauer first met in the apartment of Max Brod on 13 August 1912, just over a hundred years ago. The novel takes its temporal impetus from this event and always returns back to it. Kafka's struggle to search for and create his own identity begins with this internal monologue in the form of his correspondence. Through this process of self-examination and search for self, embodied within the compulsive need to write, the endless flow of correspondence, and the production of texts, Kafka's own life was changed. And his literary world took a decisive turn as a result of his meeting Felice. The multitude of letters travelling continually: between Prague and Berlin, Eastern Europe and Europe, in the postal carriage of the Prague-Berlin railway route. The novel also evokes the half-legendary son of Kafka's, possibly born to Grete Bloch. Kafka's son becomes an allegorical figure in the novel.

The title of the novel is itself emblematic: an emblem of Eastern European fate and thought. In one sense, it is a contemplation of the fact that we Eastern Europeans are all Kafka's sons. Kafka, in a spiritual sense, inspired the most significant texts of the twentieth century. Among them are the novels and essays of Imre Kertész, whom I know personally, and who, as a writer, I look up to as my paragon.

The personal strands in the novel connect to my own life story. I was born on 1 November 1963, in a village in eastern Hungary of some 400 souls, and I grew up in Túrricse. In this tiny village, close to the Ukrainian and Romanian borders, the one-time peasant world of Eastern Europe lived on. There existed in that milieu a unique mixture of collectivist ideology and the traditional peasant worldview; at the same time, the socialist dictatorship was slowly yet gradually abating. My family were considered to be 'class enemies', and due as well to suspicions of Jewish origin, we were shunned. For me, the functionality of the collectivity of the village made the culture of brutality palpable. I attempted to explore these influences in my novel *Has the Meshiyah Left Already?* (2012).[1] In a milieu such as this, the process of growing up and the acquisition of language to do not occur within the framework of education but rather within that of a kind of harsh training, like that of for animals. *Brutally trained language usage* preserved the traditionally ancient peasant culture of brutality.

In the course of writing my novel dealing with the traumas of childhood, I came to the realization that due to the influence of the ideology of the Enlightenment, the practices of the civilization of brutality had abated everywhere in Europe, but continued to survive in Eastern Europe. Elsewhere, these practises were obscured through the means of humanization, but in Eastern Europe the still extant peasant world preserved the practices of brutal upbringing, employing these tools which I term as *brutal training*.

My novel *Kafka's Son* explores these worlds which live on as hidden springs. My aim is to attempt a literary mapping of these worlds which will demonstrate, within the functionality of language, the bequeathing of

---

1 Szilárd Borbély, *Nincstelenek: Már elment a Mesijás?* (Bratislava: Kalligram, 2013).

linguistic practice, and in language acquisition itself, the brutalities that continue to exist below the surface of the concept of the nation-state stemming from the Enlightenment and other subsequent humanising societal practices.

As in *Berlin-Hamlet*, Borbély relies upon Kafka's writings, citing them within the context of his own work (in that earlier volume, he cited passages from Kafka's letters). In *Kafka's Son*, he employs two letters to Felice, one written on 27 October 1912, and the other on the night of 2 to 3 December 1912, as well as composing a letter to Felice not based on any of Kafka's actual letters. In addition, in this novel, Hermann Kafka replies to his son's letter, which in historical fact he never received. Here he gains the right of reply, to 'have his own voice and story,' as Gábor Schein puts it.[2] These letters from Hermann to Franz, interspersed through the novel, are an extended meditation on the fraught father-son relationship, itself a major theme in Hungarian letters ever since the 1970s. As Schein writes: 'Kafka, for Szilárd Borbély, is not just a personality created through writing, but a medium that Borbély animates, using Kafka as a person and a form, allowing him to talk about himself.' Indeed, a deeper analogy comes into view when we consider Borbély's 'auto-fictional' novel *The Dispossessed*, and his own troubled relationship with his father (whose death in 2006 is hauntingly described in his verse collection *In a Bucolic Land*). Hermann Kafka states, early on in *Kafka's Son*:

---

2 Gábor Schein, 'Rettenetes súly' [A dreadful weight], *Élet és irodalom* 65(32) (13 August 2021).

The father is the grave of the son.

The son is life of the father. The father is the death of the son.

Towards the end of the novel, Hermann states:

Your life is my death, I see this. Although you have said that it is because of me that you cannot live.

As Schein states, this is a paraphrase of a sentence from Imre Kertész's *Kaddish for an Unborn Child*, 'considering my existence as the possibility of your existence,' repeated in passages where he considers his refusal, as a Holocaust survivor, to engender a child, and yet addresses that very child.[3]

Kafka's Son takes place in the short time period after the Prague Jewish ghetto had been demolished—in its greatest extent between 1896 and 1903—but before all the new buildings were complete; in other words, in the period before the First World War (although the fragments do not follow a chronological order). The 'redevelopment' of the Prague ghetto (dating roughly to the early thirteenth century, hence one of the oldest Jewish ghettos in Europe) had been the goal of Prague urban planners as early as the mid-nineteenth century. Hygienic conditions in the ghetto, as well as overcrowding and lack of plumbing, were regularly cited as justification for redevelopment, or in the parlance of the age, the disturbingly bland Latinate terms of

---

3 Imre Kertész, *Kaddis a meg nem született gyermekért* (Budapest: Magvető kiadó, 1990), p. 12. Available in English as *Kaddish for an Unborn Child* (Tim Wilkinson trans.) (New York: Vintage International, 2004).

Sanierung or *asanace*.[4] Between the swelling currents of anti-Semitism in the last decades of Habsburg rule, the desire of a nationalist-minded Czech bourgeoisie for a suitably imposing metropolis, and an emerging, often highly assimilationist, Jewish middle class with a notably ambiguous stance toward its own recent past (as, indeed, Kafka himself was often painfully aware), it was no surprise that this unique urban organism was levelled in favour of today's logical street-grid and elegant Secessionist apartment blocks. In grim irony, the most vocal defenders of the old Prague ghetto, alongside the artists and preservationists defending its aesthetic qualities, were often the era's most anti-Semitic elements.[5]

By the outbreak of the First World War—when, to cite Kafka's famous diary entry, he noted Germany's declaration of war and his afternoon swimming with equal importance—even the ruins and empty lots of the ghetto's destruction had almost entirely vanished. Four years of bloodshed, in turn, gave way to the dissolution of the Habsburg empire, with Prague now the capitol of an independent Czechoslovak state, and Czech the official language in Bohemia and Moravia. The German-Czech linguistic and national tensions, both before and after 1918 are evident in *Kafka's Son*: one of Kafka's bosses insists on addressing him as *Herr*, as opposed to Czech *pan*, insisting on his 'Germanness'. And

---

4 Strangely, the secret police of Communist Czechoslovakia also used 'Asanace' as the internal designation for their campaign to drive dissidents into exile in the late 1970s and early 80s.

5 For an English-language analysis of these events, see Cathleen Giustino, *Tearing Down Prague's Jewish Town: Ghetto Clearance and the Legacy of Middle-Class Ethnic Politics around 1900* (Boulder, CO: East European Monographs, 2003).

the Jewish citizenry of the new state now found themselves confronted with having to make a deliberate choice of language-community. Throughout the centuries-long history of the Jewish presence in Prague, 'Jews were feared and despised, but also needed';[6] now, the situation grew even more complicated, particularly for Prague's German-speakers.[7] Kafka was, of course, conversant in Czech but only wrote it in occasional correspondence; the Yiddish of the travelling theatre troupes he admired and the Hebrew of the growing Zionist movement were strong presences in his awareness, yet it was German that formed not only the basis of his literary work but equally his professional career (and, by extension, personal and financial independence). Here, the still grimmer ironies of a German-Jewish creative identity in the twentieth century merely lay in a future that Kafka—all too fortunately—never lived to see, yet (much as in Borbély's earlier treatment in *Berlin-Hamlet*) they cannot but overshadow how we imagine, or even read, it today.

In the grant proposal that forms his most extensive and, to my knowledge, his only personal discussion of the present work, Borbély wrote of his project not merely as the writing of a novel but also as a wider philosophical examination of the culture of brutality spanning the bounds of geography and time. He clearly saw a strong connection between the brutality he suffered as a small child in the tiny village of Túrricse in north-western

6 Reiner Stach, *Kafka: The Early Years* (Shelley Frisch trans.) (Princeton, NJ: Princeton University Press), p. 17.

7 For an overview of the Jewish situation within the Czech lands at this period, see Kateřina Čapková and Hillel J. Kieval (eds), *Prague and Beyond: Jews in the Bohemian Lands* (Philadelphia: University of Pennsylvania Press, 2021).

Hungary, the brutality that Kafka was subjected to by his own father, and the generalized brutality and strictly authoritarian nature of Hapsburg society. The deep generosity of his authorial vision meant that he could never look upon Hermann Kafka, or indeed his own father, as a mere tyrant, but rather as a similar victim of the same culture of brutality. Borbély's grant project remained unfinanced and, if we can even speak of its having been realized at all, still more fragmentary than his manuscript of *Kafka's Son*. Yet in an *oeuvre* cut short by his own tragedy, he left behind a no-less-significant contribution: the fragment as suggestion, as indication, as invitation to reflect.

* * *

I would like to acknowledge the invaluable assistance of Jenő Gál, who helped me with some of the more enigmatic passages and who has been a steadfast support over many years; Péter Rácz of the Hungarian Translators' House in Balatonfüred, Hungary, where I completed both in-person and virtual residencies while working on the translation, the friendship and support of both Ágnes Mészáros and Gábor Schein; and everyone at Seagull Books, for making this publication possible, but especially Sunandini Banerjee for her magnificent work and Bishan Samaddar for his careful stewardship of the text.

TRANSLATOR'S NOTES

p. 6. *Then, gathering all of his strength, and conquering all of his natural fears, in 1914 . . . he asked for Felice's hand,*: The text breaks off here.

p. 7. *In independent Czechoslovakia, after the war*: Czechoslovakia was granted independence in 1918.

p. 21. *We see Kafka step out the entrance of the apartment building known as 'Zum Schiff'*: Known in Czech as the Dům U Lodi, this building was located at the end of Niklasstraße (Mikulášská třída), later renamed Pariser Straße (Pařížská), or Paris Street. Located at No. 36 on the bank of the Vltava, it was partially destroyed during bombing in the Second World War and then razed; in the early 1970s, the Hotel Intercontinental was completed on the site.

p. 21. *Kafka stepped out of the building standing at the corners of Niklasstraße and XXX*: The building would have been located at the corner of Niklasstraße and Dvořák Quai (Dvořákovo nábřeží).

p. 21. *[The house] had been built*: In the manuscript, the presumed subject of the sentence 'the house' is omitted, and the sentence appears to be incomplete.

p. 22. *the young Franz Josef*: The continuation of this thought in the sentence is unclear.

p. 22. *considering Batthányi's rank, however, he was not to be hanged*: Count Lajos Batthyány de Németújvár (1807–1849), the first prime minister of Hungary. He was executed by firing squad in Pest on 6 October 1849.

p. 25. *Rudolf Park*: Today Chotkovy sady (Chotek Gardens).

p. 26. *the newly built Prager Repräsentationshaus*: Today known as Obecní dům (Municipal House).

p. 27. *Ziegenleichenstraße*: The manuscript contains the word *Ziegenleinchenstraße*. As the German translators note, the word Borbély probably intended was *Ziegenleichenstraße*, 'Goat Corpse Street'. Szilárd Borbély, *Kafkas Sohn* (Heike Flemming and Lacy Kornitzer trans) (Berlin: Suhrkamp, 2017), p. 137.

p. 29. *It was inconceivable, on the night before Yom Kippur [. . .] for he had hardly set foot in there all year long*: These two sentences somewhat repeat each other.

p. 30. *but of course he wasn't the only one who . . . this death shroud*: This sentence appears to be incomplete.

p. 30. *So be it: the details could be discussed more thoroughly during prayers*: This sentence is incomplete.

p. 34. *The rabbi perhaps knew, [. . .] he measured this man's*: Text breaks off.

p. 37. *A trip he was obliged to make, to Leitmeritz*: Litoměřice, a town in the north-western part of the Czech Republic.

p. 41. *For Felice, her work at the offices of Lingenström & Co., executed in the same self-denying manner*: This first clause in this sentence appears to be incomplete.

p. 44. *moustache trainer*: A device to shape the way a moustache grows.

p. 47. *Days of Repentance*: This is the period between Rosh Hashanah and Yom Kippur.

p. 50. *Kafka stepped out of the building known as 'Zum Schiff' on the corner of Niklasstraße and Josephsplatz*: This building would have been located at the corner of Niklasstraße and Johannesplatz (formerly Jánské náměstí, now Náměstí Curieových). Josefsplatz is one of the former designations for Náměstí Republiky (Republic Square).

p. 51. *There are only conjurers and the gullible*: This sentence is followed by two percentage signs in the original, presumably a typo.

p. 51. *although he could send this trip to the devil*: A full stop is missing after this sentence, although the next sentence begins with a capital letter.

p. 55. *he wept when the young calves were slammed in the head with the shochet's hammer*: A shochet is a Jewish ritual slaughterer. As Gábor Schein has noted, the detail about the shochet's hammer is inaccurate (personal communication).

p. 56. *if, though, there were no goyim in the shop, but only his fellow Jews, he continued the pilpul*: The explanation of Talmudic texts.

p. 58. *above the park named for Crown Prince Rudolf and the winding paths of the Belvedere*: Today known as Královská zahrada (Royal Garden of Prague Castle) and Letohrádek královny Anny (Queen Anne's Summer Palace).

p. 58. *they would be moving from the house 'Zu den drei Königen'*: Located on Zeltnergasse (today Celetná) 3.

p. 59. *From his room, Kafka* [...] *the empty lot in front of the apartment building, Josephsplatz*: Text breaks off.

p. 61. *In this way, my late appearance—for nine o'clock had passed already—did not bode well*: This section, until the end of this chapter, is an extended quotation from Kafka's letter to Felice, dated 27 October 1912. The author cites the Hungarian translation contained in *Franz Kafka: Naplók, levelek. Válogatás* (László Antal,

István Eörsi and Dezső Tandori trans) (Budapest: Európa Könyvkiadó, 1981), pp. 120–25. My translation follows the version used by Borbély, with some minor amendments.

p. 63. *I recall the name of Fény*: This appears to be a typo (*fény*, 'light') which should read as 'Ferry'.

p. 65. *Nornepygge Castle*: *The Novel of the Indifferent* [*Schloss Nornepygge: Der Roman des Indifferenten*], by Max Brod, was published in 1908.

p. 66. *In Perlgasse*: Today, Perlová ulice.

p. 67. *On Obstgasse and the Graben*: Today, Ulice 28. října and Na příkopě, respectively.

p. 67. *how you took tea in the Repräsentationshaus across from the hotel*: The author appended a note to himself in the text in square brackets concerning the Repräsentationshaus (today known as Obecní dům, or Municipal House), noting its function as the 'Representative house' of Prague, its location and that it contained a restaurant, coffee house and ballrooms.

p. 68. *Clearly you thought you would be departing from the Franz Josef Bahnhof*: Today known as Praha hlavní nádraží.

p. 72. *The outside of the envelope reveals nothing*: The author cites Kafka's letter to Felice, dated from the evening of 2 to 3 December 1912 (*Franz Kafka: Naplók, levelek*, pp. 191–2).

p. 76. *through the Kleinseite*: Today known as Malá Strana, the area below Prague Castle.

p. 96. *His doubts were connected to the faith of the Jews in the very least, the Christians*: Text breaks off.

p. 96. *The lines, whether they be straight or curved*: Text breaks off.

p. 96. *when there are no longer any ghettos in Prague*: In the late nineteenth century, Prague city planners decided to redevelop Josefstadt (Josefov), the historical Jewish district in the centre of Prague. This urban planning project, known as *asanace* ('redevelopment, renewal'), presumably necessitated by poor hygienic conditions, lack of plumbing and overcrowding, took place during the years 1893–1913. Many Czech artists, writers and architects, aware of the historical and architectural importance of Josefov, protested in an attempt to halt its destruction. Eventually, however, new and wider streets were installed to replace the narrow winding alleys, and the preponderance of residential buildings were razed and replaced with large apartment blocks; synagogues and ceremonial halls were for the most part preserved.

p. 98. *Großer Ring*: Also known as the Altstädter Ring, or today, as Staroměstské náměstí (Old Town Square).

The opening paragraphs of this section are a close variation of the opening sections of 'The Fart'.

p. 99. *The stubborn and hopeless cases*: This sentence fragment seems clearly to refer to the kinds of insurance cases that the porter chased away.

p. 101. *He went to his newest studio, located in the Goldenes Gäßchen*: This sentence seems to be a variation of the one before it. Goldenes Gäßchen is today known as Zlatá ulička.

p. 102. *On Niklasstraße, this recently constructed boulevard built in the New Style, [...] more precisely it reminded them of the lovely former scenes of their lives*: This appears to be an incomplete sentence.

p. 103. *On that evening he was completely close to something, the irresolvable contradictions*: Incomplete sentence.

p. 104. *Why am I so fascinated with the story of Nebuchadnezzar*: In the Bible, Nebuchadnezzar was responsible for destroying Solomon's Temple, thus initiating the Babylonian captivity.

p. 105. *In the sunlight [ ], which he'd brought here from distant mountains*: The author inserted a space after 'In the sunlight'; the referent of 'which' is not entirely clear.

p. 110. *a refreshing breeze from the direction of Niklas Bridge*: Today known as Čechův Most.

p. 111. *The residents of Prague call Niklasstraße the 'suicides' ramp'*: Benjamin Ross, the translator of Kafka's complete diaries, notes: 'In late October 1907, when only the approach road but not the bridge (the Svatopluk Čechbrücke) itself had been finished, Kafka called Niklasstraße the approach road for suicides.' *The Diaries / Franz Kafka* (Benjamin Ross trans.) (New York: Schocken Books, 2022), p. 560. Kafka wrote to Hedwig Weiler in 1908: 'Last week I really belonged in this street I live on, which I call "Suicide Lane," for the street traces a broad path down to the river; there a bridge is being built... For the present, however, only the framework of the bridge has been erected; the street stops at the river. But all this is only a joke, for it will always be finer to go across the bridge to the Belvedere than to go through the river into heaven.' Franz Kafka, *Letters to Friends, Family, and Editors* (Richard and Clara Winston trans) (New York: Schocken Books, 1977), p. 55. See also Veronika Tuckerová, 'Kafka a mosty,' Pocta železničnímu mostu, *Bubínek Revolveru* (June 2023): 19.

p. 112. *looks towards Josefplatz*: This would have been Johannesplatz.

p. 134. Auf wiedersehen *or* Dobrý den: The author wrote the phonetic equivalent of the Slovak greeting *Dobrý deň* in his manuscript. The Czech expression is *Dobrý den*, which means 'Good day' ('goodbye' is *Na shledanou*).

p. 138. *We see Kafka as he crosses the Old Town Square*: The opening sections of this chapter repeat passages from the chapter entitled 'A Cloudy Day'.

p. 146. *Namely, the story, as once someone* [ ]: Incomplete clause.

p. 150. *The Civil Servant*: An earlier version of this chapter contains the author's note that this section depicts Franz telling Milena about his last day at the Insurance Institute. *Kafka fia* (Budapest: Jelenkor Kiadó , 2021), p. 169.

p. 151. *deliberately and warningly using the word* Herr *instead of* pan: *pan* is 'Mr' in Czech.

p. 154. *the western . . . corner of the Großer Ring*: Ellipsis in the text.

p. 154. *and that this attention* [ ] *me*: Text breaks off.

p. 155. *Perhaps ever since your siblings Georg and Hermann died*: The name of the second sibling of Franz's to die in childbirth was Heinrich.